SILENCING THE SIREN

AN EVER AFTER MYSTERY

DENISE L. BARELA

ISBN: 978-1-951839-45-1

Celebrate Lit Publishing

304 S. Jones Blvd #754

Las Vegas, NV, 89107

http://www.celebratelitpublishing.com/

PROLOGUE

Andrew paced back and forth, tugging at his blond hair. She couldn't be dead. Impossible! He'd just seen Annabel earlier that week! How could she be gone so suddenly?

They'd gone around the island and spent time just sitting on the beach. She had spent the whole time smiling and seemed so happy. It had been one of his favorite days spent with her. No worries, no interference, and nothing but the love they shared. Even more, it had been the first day for some time that Andrew felt truly carefree.

Now his future had just disintegrated overnight.

Andrew thought back on their final conversation. Her eyes had been bright when she kissed him goodbye and said she couldn't wait for his next visit. But there had been that fidgeting nervousness that had consumed her for those few minutes.

She'd said she had a surprise for him.

What surprise had she been talking about? Surely, this wasn't it.

Something was wrong about the whole situation, but

Andrew couldn't imagine what it could be. How could she be there one day and gone the next? Nothing made sense.

Thoughts rushed through his head, drowning him in grief and misery. But one question forced its way into every thought: how could this have happened?

He would find the answer, although he had no clue where to start. He needed to know what led to her death. Needed to know who killed her and why they picked her as their victim. Did her kind heart make her an easy target? Could it be because of him?

He would solve this… well, mystery! And he'd make sure the criminals were held responsible. Make sure they were brought to justice. It was the least he could do for her. Maybe it would serve as a way to distract himself from the pain of her loss and the void she left behind in his heart.

His Annabel didn't deserve this fate. She deserved the world and everything in it, but he couldn't give it to her now. Anger clashed and rolled with the grief inside him. A war of fire and ice with no clear winner.

He would solve this mystery and would find her killer.

Even if it was the last thing he'd ever do.

They, whoever "they" were, wouldn't get away with it.

ONE

Andrew tiptoed quietly through the house. He wasn't sure if his parents were home, and he'd rather avoid any confrontation with them today. The Graysons were one of the wealthiest families with a townhome not that far from Central Park. Any other day, Andrew would be found there with his pals goofing around, but not today. Today, he was determined to finally make it to Coney Island. All his friends had managed to visit the once glamorous resort, but since the opening of the new subway, his parents had forbidden him from going and getting caught up with the "riffraff," as his parents called them. Andrew didn't have much of an opinion in that area.

Grabbing his hat off the coat rack, Andrew slipped out the front door and onto the sidewalk. The cool crisp air blowing in from the sea greeted him as he tugged his suit jacket a little tighter around his lean frame. On the brisk walk to the subway, Andrew was quite glad that no one stopped him on his way to the station. The last thing he needed was to be questioned on his destination.

The row of townhouses once impressed and dazzled Andrew, but he had grown rather weary of the sight by now.

He longed for excitement and something new. He'd been told the attraction that had popped up on Coney Island would provide just that. Envy had burrowed itself in his heart when all his friends spoke of the place and all their experiences. No matter how much he had tried convincing his parents to allow him to go, they wouldn't budge. Desperate times called for desperate measures. He was forced to an abrupt stop when two children ran across his path. Andrew smiled at their laughter as they passed by him. How he longed to experience those days at least once more. Back when life was about all the toys his parents would buy him to keep him happy. He had been a boy who wanted for nothing because he had everything. Even now, Andrew's parents bought him everything he wanted within reason. Although it had taken him a few weeks to convince them to buy him a car, they caved in the end.

Andrew Grayson was a spoiled, rich boy in every sense of the word, though he didn't exactly flaunt it. Okay, maybe he did flaunt it. Anyhow, people knew his situation and wanted a part of it. At the start of it all, Andrew adored the attention lavished upon him. As time went on, he began to notice the lack of loyalty in those he had deemed his friends. This left a gaping hole in his heart. Was it so wrong to want friends that liked him for who he was rather than how high his society standing reached?

The corners of his mouth turned down, and Andrew turned back around to face the subway. He kept a brisk pace to avoid being late, but he also didn't want to ruin his image by running all the way to the platform. That wouldn't be very becoming of a gentleman.

He slipped himself into an empty seat at the back of the subway and removed his hat. He set it on his lap before taking in his surroundings. All around him were people his parents always warned him against associating with. However, Andrew was never one to give much care to the rules his parents established. It wasn't that he meant to be rebellious.

Well, maybe he did, but it wasn't that difficult to do given the number of rules set in place. He could breathe wrong, and they'd be right there to correct him on how to properly breathe. It was a wonder he hadn't suffocated yet.

But Andrew loved being around people. While the lingering superiority existed within him, he couldn't find it within himself to be rude to the lower classes like his parents could. His friends all acted the same as well. Trying to fit in at those moments was painful for Andrew. He'd wanted nothing more than to help up the man his friends knocked over and ensure he wasn't injured. But that would mean immediate ridicule, and the information would no doubt be passed along to his parents. That was the last thing he needed right now.

A small smile overtook his features as he watched a mother fixing her daughter's dress and telling her how much fun they were going to have. Andrew hoped he could say the same for himself. His mother would never have brought him on something like this as a child unless the price point meant the lower classes couldn't afford to ride. Then she would have been keen on it. He resisted the desire to roll his eyes. Mother missed out on so much with her prejudices.

Even at a young age, her presence in his life was as minimal as she could get away with. Seeing moments between a parent and child like the one just now always drove home the loss he felt deep down at the lack of connection with his parents. Their definition of a parent-child relationship consisted of telling him what to do and throwing gifts his way when he wanted something.

It was the same every birthday. All he wanted was to spend an evening with his parents, at the very least have dinner with them. Every year he begged them for at least a week to go out for his birthday. They told him they would do their best. Eventually, he just stopped asking. The reminder dropped his mood some. He glanced out the window and watched the buildings speed by.

The ride was relatively smooth, which gave Andrew a lot of time to think. He was impressed at the level of comfort the subway provided for such a low cost. The rumble of the wheels on the track brought a calm to Andrew's mind, and the vibration from the movement of the subway lulled him into a gentle sleep.

Andrew didn't know how long he'd been asleep when someone was shaking him awake.

"Sir, we've arrived," a man said in a soft tone.

Andrew opened his eyes and looked around. The subway car stood empty of its previous passengers. An elderly gentleman leaned over him with a kind smile. The young man returned the smile and thanked him before getting up from his seat. He stepped off the subway and onto the station platform at Coney Island. He followed the crowd through the station toward the hub of the tourist attraction ahead. It was loud and packed with people.

When he reached the giant sign announcing the start of the fair, he stopped and gazed up at it in awe.

He was finally here.

Andrew made his way down the dusty street, attention pulled in many different directions. Coney Island was every bit what his friends described. Lights strung up across the tents bathed the island in their magical glow. The smells of the various delicacies wafted around him. But one stood out. It was an earthy, savory scent. A large sign hung in front of him with the word "Popcorn" in large print. The foreign aroma lured him in, a hint of butter adding to the temptation. After handing the man ten cents for the small, he took his first bite.

It was unlike anything he had ever tasted before. The butter, the salt, and the popcorn blended together in perfect harmony.

He munched on his new favorite snack as he observed the people milling around playing games, riding the attractions, and lining up for a rather large tent sitting at the end of the boardwalk. The red and white stripes clashed against the blue behind it. Shouting from the front of the crowd stole his attention, though he could not understand what the person said. Weaving through the throng of people, Andrew moved closer to the shouting man.

"Come one, come all!" The man waved his hands around and gestured to the tent behind him. "Come in and see the freakish wonders the world has to offer!"

The crowd murmured and pushed toward the tent. Andrew's interest was piqued. What surprises did it hold inside? He followed the herd in and took in the view. Wooden benches were tiered around the circular stage in the center of the canvas.

"Ladies and gentlemen! If you take your seats, we can get started with our show!"

Andrew rushed to his seat and watched the man in red waiting in the middle of the ring, baton in hand. Music blared and performers rushed forward. Their bodies spun and twirled around each other, voices came together in harmony and excited the crowd.

Andrew smiled wide at the scene before him. The troupe had various acts that kept both him and the other audience members on the edge of their seats. Andrew felt faint when the "Giant Man" stepped on to the stage.

"Now everyone, we have saved the best for last. Mothers, I only ask that you keep your daughters in their seats. We have reached the final act of our performance. I present to you, the Beauty of the Seven Seas, Our Irish Mermaid, Saoirse!"

The crew rolled out a large tank full of water, but it was what resided in the tank that made Andrew's lungs deflate like a balloon.

A girl, no older than seventeen, Andrew guessed, was floating in the water. Her long red hair made it look as though she were on fire. Her skin was fair, and Andrew longed to know if it was as soft as it looked. He could not see her eyes, but there was no doubt in his mind that they would add to her beauty. As she began to move, he realized why they called her a mermaid. Where her legs should have been was a shining purple tail. She lifted her head, showing off vibrant green eyes.

Andrew drew in a deep breath as they made eye contact. Her pale skin brought out the color of her hair and eyes. He had never seen anyone as exotic and beautiful as her. He smiled and watched as she continued her routine. Arms swayed gracefully as she moved to the music, perfectly in time with the band off to the side of the stage. Andrew was completely enraptured with her; the way her hair shone under the light swirling around her as she moved, her skin glowed like pearls, and her tail sparkled like thousands of tiny diamonds.

Her eyes made their way back to him, and she gave him a small smile. Andrew couldn't help the large smile that spread across his face in return. The music had faded away. All Andrew knew right then was her. She was everything in that one moment. Despite being able to hear his parents' objections in his head, Andrew wanted a future with her. It was everything he ever wanted.

Clapping pulled Andrew from his thoughts. The woman who had overrun his thoughts had vanished as if part of the act. The crowd was leaving their seats and making their way to the exit, but he didn't want to leave yet. He had to meet her.

Andrew joined the line as they filed out of the tent. He adjusted the hat on his head and gave a gentle tug to his suit jacket.

"A gentleman must always look his best," his mother's constant chiding echoed in his mind.

The top of the tent gave way to the sunny sky. The mist from the ocean felt cool against his skin, warmed from the amount of people in the tent. Andrew weaved through the

various tents offering different commodities and vying for his attention. A time or two he was tempted to stop and browse the watches and other shiny trinkets offered, but he kept himself on task.

As Andrew passed by one of the smaller tents along the outskirts of the fair, a sudden force knocked into him and crushed his feet. A rather ungentlemanly yelp escaped his lips and he whipped around to face the culprit. The scolding died on his lips as his gaze landed on her. The one he had been seeking.

"I-I'm so s-sorry!" The girl wheeled herself forward. "I meant no offense or harm. I thought there was enough space for me to fit there!"

Andrew could only stare. She was so much more beautiful up close than when she was performing on the stage. Her voice was just as lovely as her face and hair.

"Sir?"

He snapped out of his reverie and gave a slight bow to the young woman before him. "The fault was mine. I should have paid better attention to where I was going." Andrew grasped her hand in his and left a gentle kiss on the back of her palm.

A soft giggle left the girl's lips at Andrew's behavior. "That's mighty sweet of you." She tucked a strand of hair behind her ear and fluttered her eyelashes. "Does this fine gentleman have a name?"

Said gentleman immediately flushed and words tumbled out of his mouth before he could stop himself. "MynameisAndrew."

The girl pressed her hand against her mouth, and her shoulders shook. "Sorry, that was unkind of me. I think you just said your name was Andrew?"

He nodded.

"A wonderful name for a handsome man. It's an honor to meet you." She gave a small bow of her head.

"You have a beautiful name too, Saoirse." He gave her a wink.

She giggled before looking around quickly, then gestured for Andrew to lean closer. He complied.

"I'll tell you a secret." She glanced around again. "My real name isn't Saoirse, it's Annabel. They gave me the name Saoirse for the show." She brushed imaginary dust off the blanket on her lap. "It sounds like the name an Irish mermaid would have."

Andrew watched her fiddle with the hem of the blanket. Being this close to her made him lose his confidence from before. "It's beautiful, um…" he rubbed the back of his neck, "…like you."

"Oh, thank you." A rosy glow spread across Annabel's face.

Silence filled the air between them, even as the people around them continued to laugh, cheer, and call out for others to look at their wares. Andrew shuffled back a bit as they both just stared at the ground.

"Why are you in a wheelchair?"

Annabel's head shot up. "My, erm, my legs aren't right." Her gaze was on anything but him. Guilt rose within Andrew.

"I'm sorry. I shouldn't have asked that. I apologize if I made you feel uncomfortable." He went to brush a hand through his hair but knocked the hat off his head instead. He scrambled to pick it up and shoved it back onto his head.

Annabel stifled her laughter behind her palm. "It's okay. I'm not uncomfortable. The question just caught me by surprise." She pulled the blanket off her lap. "My mother told me to never be ashamed of them. God made me like this for a reason. Who am I to question it?" She smiled. "Though I do sometimes find myself praying for normal legs."

Andrew's eyes flitted from Annabel's face to her legs, then back up again. He smiled. "I love your outlook on life."

They could have stayed like this for hours, just enjoying each other's company, but good things must come to an end.

"Annabel! The next show starts in fifteen minutes! Don't be late!" One of the other performers called from the tent behind her.

Annabel held out her hand to Andrew, "It's been a lot of fun! Thank you for staying and talking to me." He grasped her hand and shook it. "It's nice being treated like a human being by someone outside of our little performing group. Catch you around!"

She wheeled herself off into the tent the other performer had just called out from.

As Andrew made his way back to the subway, only one thought permeated the thoughts of the woman he had just met.

I will most definitely return.

TWO

And return he did. Andrew couldn't keep himself away. Her face always broke into a smile whenever he found her after a show, and that smile sent his heart racing. Spending time with Annabel became his favorite pastime. He didn't just spend time with her though; she had introduced him to the other performers as well. They were much like a giant family.

Annabel had convinced her father to call a family meeting within the big tent that housed them all between shows. They all looked so different, and yet, they were also the same. Pain from the rejection they suffered at society's hands lingered in their countenances. Andrew had no doubt the people in this tent had been treated harshly over the years. There was more to them than that though. Andrew had learned that quickly and had grown to appreciate that about them. Despite the pain they endured, they still had an immense love to give to those who respected them. He'd witnessed it a few times since he began seeing Annabel. The group was such a close knit one; they'd do anything for each other and would keep one another safe at all costs.

He suspected this was the reason for some of the suspicious glances directed at him. He felt like a scolded child under their cautious gaze. Everywhere they went, someone was watching them.

Even as they made their way to the tent. He held the fabric flap open for her so she could enter without any difficulty. She gave him a small smile as she passed him.

Annabel wheeled herself in front of the group then spun around to face Andrew.

"This is my family." She gestured to the group that congregated next to her. "I'll introduce them to you!"

The ringmaster stepped forward and placed his hand on the back of Annabel's chair. "This is my father, William. He's the leader of our merry band of misfits." She tilted her head up to look at her father. "He takes good care of us."

The others joined in with a chorus of agreement. A few of them patted him on the back.

"If there's anything you want to know about our traveling group, just come and find me." William gave a small bow and a laugh. "After seeing the care with which you treat her, you're more than welcome here whenever you'd like to visit."

Andrew gave a tip of his hat. "Thank you, sir."

Annabel tilted her head back and smiled up at her father. "He's really kind and smart. He taught me how to read as soon as I was old enough to!" She grabbed the book she had tucked next to her in the wheelchair. "I love reading. I've visited so many different places through the books I have."

Andrew smiled at her; the childlike wonder in her eyes made him want to take her to all the countries that she wanted to visit from her books. The women in his social circle never seemed to care about much beyond the latest fashion, celebrities, or the local gossip. Sometimes it was the three of them combined. What celebrities were going out with who, and what celebrities were wearing what. It all got so boring—so superficial.

But not her. His weekly visits never brought boredom or

disinterest. He was so utterly enraptured with her that time seemed to just fly by.

"Up next is Jorgen!" Annabel announced.

A man at least six inches taller than Andrew stepped forward. If the man's height wasn't intimidating enough, the way the muscles in his arms bulged most definitely was. Andrew had no doubt that this man could crush his skull if he wanted to.

"It's nice to meet you," Jorgen said, German accent thick with each word. He stuck his hand out for the lad to shake. A small part of Andrew wanted to decline for the health and safety of his hand, but he didn't want to be rude. Andrew gripped Jorgen's outstretched hand and shook it.

Jorgen let go, smirking at the boy. "Our Little Mermaid seems quite taken with you. Please take care of her."

Andrew and Annabel flushed at his words.

"Jorgen!"

The man chuckled before stepping back with the others. Next, a woman with sparse patches of facial hair stepped forward.

"I'm Amalia! Annabel is like a daughter to me." She greeted him and pressed a quick kiss to each side of his face before pulling away.

Andrew blinked at the woman, startled by the action. He smiled and gave a tilt of his head. "It's a pleasure to meet you."

"She's quite smitten with you, young man." Amalia winked at him.

A small whine sounded from behind him, and he turned to find Annabel with her face hidden in her hands.

Amalia laughed and shook her head before taking her leave too. Andrew watched as Annabel talked with Levi, who had a snake curled around his arm. He looked around, envy coursing through his veins at how close the whole group was. He marveled again at how he'd missed this level of closeness with his family, despite being related by blood. Most considered that the strongest bond there was, but not for his family. And not for the one in front of him either. This family was put together purely by the love and friendship they had for each other. The love they had ran far deeper than the blood Andrew shared with his parents.

And Annabel. He knew what his people thought of these types of people. How often they were looked down on by those in high society. There was so much more to each of these performers than any of his friends would ever realize. His world would shun the very girl that made him feel like he could be himself. That thought made Andrew's heart clench tightly. What would they do if they ever found out how attached he was? Drag him away? Lock him up?

The soft calling of his name drew him from his reverie. Annabel wheeled herself over to his side and smiled up at him. "You look a little lost there." She giggled and nudged his arm. "What's got your attention?"

The word was out of his mouth before he could stop it. "You." His eyes widened and his cheeks flushed. "I can't believe I just said that." Andrew looked away from her, mortification consuming him.

"Hey."

His gaze shifted down to Annabel.

She tucked a small strand of hair behind her ear, observing him. Her eyes were hidden beneath her long lashes. "You're quite funny, Mr. Andrew."

He groaned. "Don't tease me. I'm already embarrassed enough as it is."

"Sorry, sorry." She gave a small laugh.

Silence surrounded them. He looked around the tent and realized everyone had gone.

"They've gone off to get ready for the next show." Annabel said.

Andrew pulled his watch from his suit jacket pocket and checked the time. "I need to catch the next subway back to the city, or my mother will have my hide when I get back."

She nodded. "I'll go with you to the subway."

Silence continued between them, but instead of the awkward silence from earlier, this one was comfortable. All around them, children and families wandered through the attractions that Coney Island had to offer. Andrew admired the view and enjoyed the antics of the visitors. He was so caught up in his own observations that he missed the sorrow-filled look that overtook Annabel's face.

Her thoughts and attention were focused elsewhere. Her gaze followed the couples or people her age as they savored the fair experiences and each other's presence. She often wondered if they knew how lucky they were. They could go wherever they wanted to, nothing physically to hold them back.

Did they know what she would give to have that same opportunity? All her life, she wished she had normal legs, prayed for normal legs. She wanted to join the children running around in the street, enjoy the feeling of sand between her toes as they ran along the beach. Even learning to swim had been extremely difficult for her. Why couldn't she just be normal?

Andrew and Annabel stopped at the entrance to the subway station, where the sound of everyone waiting to board made it difficult for them to hear what the other tried to say. Andrew kneeled down in front of Annabel and leaned in so they could converse much more easily.

"Thank you for today. I'm glad you could come visit me." Annabel's fingers tugged at the hem of her sweater. "It's nice to have a friend outside of my little family."

Andrew gave her a genuine smile and reached out for her

hands. He gave them a gentle squeeze as he spoke. "I always have a great time when I'm with you."

Her face flamed at his words. She smoothed the sweater against her thighs. "Andrew, I—"

The last call sounded out from the subway behind her.

"I have to go. I'll see you soon, Annabel!" He took off for the subway before she could even respond.

Andrew made his way to the back of the subway car and looked out the window, giving her a small wave and a smile.

Annabel gave a slow wave as the subway left the station. "I've never had this much fun with anyone before…"

She sighed and wheeled herself back to the tents. Her next show started soon.

THREE

Andrew stared down out the window while he fiddled with the hat resting in his lap. The subway ambled along the track at its moderate pace. Every time he visited the island, it got harder and harder to leave. His desire to stay grew more each time. He lost count of his trips after the first week of visiting his little mermaid. *I wish I could just run away from all the falseness of this life, and just join Annabel and her merry crew.* Right now, he'd never look back.

If someone had told his younger self that he would ever be willing to give up his wealth and status to join a side attraction on Coney Island, there would have been quite the scuffle. He never imagined spending days on end sitting next to a fake mermaid or congregating with her family as they all spent time reading a chapter of the Bible each morning. Religion had never been important to him or his parents, but now, he was beginning to reconsider when he listened and watched them. It was a whole new concept, and he was more than curious to know more about it. Despite the less-than-favorable living conditions, those part of the traveling show were rarely without a smile.

The hum and motion of the subway as it made its way

back to the city soothed Andrew as he contemplated what awaited him at home. He'd been too careless as of late. It was only a matter of time before they caught on to his strange behavior.

His parents grew more and more suspicious of his disappearances every time they happened. Apparently, the servants weren't on his side. The snitches. Either he had to come up with a good cover story or just come clean about where he'd been. He didn't relish either option. His parents knew him well enough to spot a lie from a mile away. Not that he'd ever been that great of a liar anyway. At the same time, telling them he'd been frequenting the Coney Island freak show opened himself up to what would no doubt be a long and tiresome lecture. Avoiding that at all costs would be the best outcome in this situation.

There was always the option of telling the half-truth, though. He's been out visiting a new friend in hopes of getting to know him a little better. It was mostly true, after all. They didn't need to know that this friend was actually a "she" and that she was a part of the freak show that settled on the small island. What they don't know won't kill them, or so the saying went, right?

A tap on the shoulder pulled Andrew from his worries. "Sir, we've arrived."

Andrew stood up and straightened out his clothing before exiting the subway. The air here was different. How he longed for the fresh air he had come to love on Coney Island.

In an attempt to delay the inevitable, Andrew opted to walk back home rather than hailing a taxi. Though he had come to learn shortcuts for the quickest route from his home to the station, he took what once was his normal route through Central Park. He could use some time to work on making his story sellable to his parents.

"Mother, Father. Lovely evening, don't you think?" He uttered to himself. Oh yes, that was sure to convince them that he wasn't up to no good. Andrew shook his head at his own stupidity. It was official now. He was doomed to suffer through one of his parents' tirades. He bit his lip. Too bad he didn't pay more attention to his friends' conversation about how to get away with things. He could use that wisdom right about now.

The air was cool and crisp now that evening had arrived, and the sun was already low in the sky. Soon, Andrew would need his thicker jacket when he went out. If he were still allowed to go out after tonight. He wasn't going to hold his breath on that. Image was everything to his family, and heaven forbid Andrew ruin what they had worked so hard for. He didn't want to be responsible for that.

Andrew tucked his hands into his pockets, looking around the park at the other visitors. He wondered if their lives were as difficult as his seemed to be. Did they have the same level of pressure on their shoulders? Were their burdens as heavy as his seemed to be? He rolled his eyes. Like his troubles were as heavy as some others were. Annabel had conjoined legs and lived in a traveling freak show. His life was nowhere near as difficult as hers was, and yet she seemed so much more care-free. He'd have to ask her secret the next time he visited.

He continued his walk through the streets, trying to extend his arrival home. He never thought he would ever tire of the view near his home. Buildings lined the streets on both sides. The sight used to fill him with excitement when he would go out with his friends. Now, all he longed for was the open view of Coney Island. Sooner than he had hoped, he arrived on his block. Rounding the corner, his house came into view. Andrew wished hard that his parents would be late and wouldn't be home. He opened the front door as gingerly as he could, but the sight in the foyer dashed any hope he had of not getting caught. Closing the door behind him, he took a deep breath before turning to face his parents. They stood before him with their arms crossed.

"Mother, Father, have a good evening?" Andrew gave his parents what he hoped was a convincing smile. The looks on their faces told him it wasn't.

"And just where have you been, young man?" His mother inquired.

Andrew lifted his right hand and scratched the back of his neck before answering her. "Well, I made a new friend recently, and I've been trying to get to know him better."

His father arched an eyebrow. "Who is this new friend?"

"Just someone from the family that moved in on the next block." Andrew gave a shrug.

Andrew's heart rate increased; what other questions did they have in store? He questioned his ability to get away with this. It didn't seem like it was working.

"Do you at least know his surname?"

Andrew shook his head. "I never asked."

His mother and father exchanged a look before sighing. They would not get any more answers out of him on this subject. With a tilt of his father's chin, Andrew was sent to his room. Boy, did he feel like a child at that moment—being sent to his room as if he was throwing a temper tantrum.

Andrew collapsed down onto his four-poster bed. He took a deep breath and closed his eyes. It could have gone worse, but it still wasn't the best outcome. He would have to be more careful from now on. Andrew opened his eyes and stared at the ceiling above him. How much longer would he be able to keep this up before his parents figured out what was going on?

Andrew decided he was tired of thinking about it and chose to retire for the evening. Maybe things would be better tomorrow. Better to face it with a clear and well-rested mind. With one final lingering thought of Annabel, he closed his eyes and succumbed to his exhaustion.

Annabel had fared some better than her new-found friend, but not by a lot. Though he was a nice boy, he held far too much mystery to be fully accepted by her group. They did not know enough about him to trust him just yet. Though she understood, Annabel's heart still felt rather heavy. She could sense the loneliness rooted deep within him, and just maybe she could be what he needed at this moment in life. Her family had always shown her so much love and kindness. She just wanted to share a little bit of that with him. She doubted he experienced much of that anywhere else.

Annabel stared down at the letter she'd received this morning. If they knew about this, they would be even more unwilling to get to know him. An envelope with what looked to be a family crest rested on her lap. A beautiful script lay across the front with her stage name on it. Whoever it was, Andrew hadn't told them her real name, so she had no reason to suspect his involvement. She took the letter out of the envelope and read it again.

STAY AWAY FROM ANDREW GRAYSON.

She had no idea who had written the note or why they wanted her to stay away from him. Was it a warning about his character or a threat to her because of her appearance? Annabel had more questions than answers, but nothing could be done right now. She pushed the letter to the back of her mind as she headed off to get ready for the next show.

Annabel wheeled herself into her tent and headed straight for her wardrobe. It would take some work, but she had no doubt that she could convince her family to accept the boy eventually. She sorted through the pile of clothes before she found the purple piece of clothing she was looking for. After having thrown the blanket off her lap and onto the bed, she shimmied into the tail and pulled it up her legs before she cinched it around her waist. Moving on land was hard for her to tackle, but water provided her a sense of normalcy that she couldn't find elsewhere.

The sound of someone clearing his throat from outside her tent caught her attention. A familiar voice floated in through the tent flap at the entrance. "Darling," her father called out.

Annabel maneuvered herself to the opening of her tent. With her left hand on the wheel of her chair to keep it steady, she reached out with her right hand to pull back one of the flaps.

"Yes, Father?" she responded.

He gave her a small smile before gesturing to her. "May I come in?"

She nodded.

He entered through the other flap and walked over to her vanity, taking a seat in the chair there.

"Are you all set for tonight's show?"

She shook her head and wheeled herself over to where her father sat. "I just have one or two more things to do and then I'll be ready."

He merely nodded at her. "I haven't just come to check on you, I must confess. As your father, I feel I must speak to you about your new friend."

Annabel internally rolled her eyes. She should have seen this coming; it was only a matter of time. "His name is Andrew. What is there to speak about?"

The girl's father gave a deep breath and ran his hand down his face. "Don't make this difficult for me, child. I only speak out of concern for you and the others in my care."

The petulant look on her face softened. "Sorry Father. I know. Please continue."

One corner of his mouth quirked up. "He's a good lad, and I know you like him very much."

She blushed. "Father!"

He held up his hands in mock surrender. "I'm not saying there's anything wrong with it. I just don't want to see you get hurt." This time, he ran a hand through his hair. "His kind of people… well, let's just say they're not exactly fond of us."

Annabel jumped in. "He's not like them, Father. He is so kind and gentle. You just have to get to know him a little bit better."

William took both of his daughter's hands in his. "You are so like your mother sometimes. She never failed to see the good in everyone she met." He gave them a squeeze. "I can see the good in him, but that doesn't mean that everything is okay. He has family and friends in high society. What will happen when they learn of his friendship with you?"

Annabel stared down at the glittery tail she wore. She'd rather not think about it, but she knew her father was right.

"It won't be him they go after when they find out." His features softened. "I'm not saying that you can't be his friend. I'm just asking that you be careful. I love you, and I don't want anything to happen to you." He leaned over and pressed a kiss to her forehead.

She gave a long, low sigh. "I know, Father. I love you too, and I'll be careful." She smiled before clapping her hands. "Well, I best finish getting ready for the show. Can't have your main attraction be late!"

He heaved a hearty laugh and ran his thumb along her cheek. "Thank you, my little one, for not making this conversation harder for me than it already was. I didn't want to hurt you."

"I know, and I'm very grateful for that. It's just hard. I really like him." Her voice cracked.

"I know, my dear. There's nothing wrong with that, but you just always want to exercise caution. Now, I'll leave you to finish getting ready. Just know that I love you." This time, he kissed her cheek before heading towards the front of her tent.

"I love you too." She gave him a genuine smile this time. As hard as it was to hear what he had to say, she knew he did it because he loved her and wanted to protect her from the harms Andrew's world held for her.

She quickly changed into her show top and ran a brush through her hair to work out any knots that may have formed in the wind. Setting aside the conflict waging war within her head, Annabel put on a smile and headed out for the performance tent. Without any trace of hesitation in her movements, Annabel performed just as well as she did any other night.

Only when she settled down to sleep did the thoughts return. Their overwhelming nature threatened to keep her awake for the whole night. Dwelling on those thoughts would do her no good right now. She could tackle it in the morning with a fresh mind, and hopefully, a better rested one.

FOUR

Andrew breathed in the New York City air as he took a walk before heading home for dinner. Well over a week had passed since he had last visited Annabel and Coney Island. Though the distance made his heart ache in ways he never experienced before, he knew it was a safer option for both of them. He needed to give his parents time to forget about his weekly absences. Putting the confrontation behind him should help make them less suspicious when he began his visits again. Though now, he didn't think he could visit as often. That was something he'd rather not think about. The island gave him a sense of freedom he couldn't find anywhere else and losing that was proving to be rather difficult for him.

Andrew was pulled from his thoughts at the sight of familiar faces up ahead. It seemed they had spotted him too.

His friends greeted him as they walked toward each other. "Hey, Andrew!" His friend gave a tip of his hat.

Andrew tipped his hat. "Hey, Charles! Fancy meeting you here."

The two men laughed and shook hands. Though they were friends, manners were still important to them.

"We haven't seen you around in a while. What have you been up to?" Charles inquired.

Andrew knew he could at least tell his friend about his visits to the little island off the coast. He left out the parts with Annabel. There was no use borrowing trouble when he could avoid it. "Well, I finally managed to sneak a trip or two to Coney Island."

Charles clapped him on the back. "Finally! I thought you were never going to experience it. Glad you got to see it at least once."

Andrew laughed. "Well, more than once."

"Ah! The experience is quite addicting, isn't it?" He smiled. "You aren't the only one though. I think James has been at least six times now." He tapped his chin, his brows furrowed in concentration.

Andrew decided not to tell his friend that he had well exceeded the amount of James' visits.

"So, since you've managed to learn the art of slinking out of the house, want to join the boys and me? We're heading out tomorrow at noon to sneak a visit," Charles invited.

Andrew did not want to embarrass himself in front of his friend, so he did not mention that he had in fact been caught sneaking out of the house. It's just that his parents were unaware of where he was sneaking off to.

Andrew gave Charles a smile. "Just tell me where to meet you all, and I'll be there."

After relaying the details of tomorrow's meeting, the men shook hands and parted ways. Andrew walked down to the various shops nearby. Perusing the various offerings, a special bracelet caught his eye. Dangling from the shiny silver chain was a small seashell charm. Without hesitation, Andrew grabbed the piece of jewelry and headed to the register.

"How much for this bracelet?" Andrew pressed.

The man at the counter gave Andrew a wide smile. "Ah,

that is a new type of bracelet made of platinum. We are selling it for $10. Quite a steal, yes?"

Andrew nearly choked at the cost. It would dip into his savings fund for summer, but the smile it would bring to Annabel's face was well worth the sacrifice. "I'll take it."

The man clapped his hands, "Wonderful, Mr. Grayson. Shall we charge it to your family's credit?"

He gave the clerk a nod. His father didn't pay much attention to what was purchased at places like this. There was enough of a variety of goods that even if his father did check, he wouldn't find it suspicious that Andrew had made a purchase here. Andrew beamed as he watched the man wrap the trinket in paper before handing it to him. Now, he just had to wait until tomorrow to be able to give it to her. Hopefully, she still wanted to see him.

Having spent enough time out of the house, Andrew made his way back before his absence seemed too suspicious. He greeted his mother as he walked toward the staircase. "Have a good day, Mother?"

She gave him a small nod before turning her focus back to the paper in front of her. "Lovely, darling. What have you been up to?"

Andrew shrugged. "I ran into Charles on my way to the shops, he invited me to hang out with our little group tomorrow. I think I'll join them. It would be nice to get out with friends." Andrew hoped his tone sounded nonchalant. He didn't want to give his mother any reason to press him about the plan for tomorrow.

His mother hummed in response. "That'll be nice, dear. What will you be doing?"

"I think they said something about going to the cinema." It was the first thing that came to Andrew's mind and not something uncommon for them to do.

His mother nodded, satisfied with his response. She waved him off and he proceeded upstairs to his room.

He only had to wait until tomorrow, then he could see his little mermaid once more. He hoped she'd like the bracelet he'd bought her. He wanted nothing more than to see a smile upon her face. Andrew sorted through some clothes in his closet, trying to decide what he wanted to wear tomorrow. He needed to fit in with his friends, but he also just wanted to be himself with her. He'd have to be careful with his friends around. Andrew was unsure if he could trust them with a secret of this magnitude. While they were rather forward with their thinking, he didn't know if they were ready to accept something like this just yet.

Andrew prayed he'd be able to pull this off without any issues.

⎯⎯⎯⎯⎯⎯

ANNABEL HAD HAD RATHER a rough week as she missed her new friend dearly. She couldn't help but wonder if maybe she had done something to frighten Andrew off, though she had no idea what that could've been. Of course, she did feel rather silly. Andrew had a life outside of Coney Island, and she couldn't expect him to spend all of his time here, regardless of the fact that he had done so the past couple weeks. Annabel sighed as she slipped on her costume for the next show. She couldn't help but hope that she'd see his face in the crowd smiling and waving at her.

She glanced at the newest letter on her dressing table. A shiver ran down her spine. It'd be something nice after receiving another letter with the same writing and crest. She still had no clue who could be sending the letters, but they were adamant about keeping her and Andrew apart. Didn't they know there was no need to threaten her? He hadn't come to visit her this past week, so why write this letter?

Hearing the front of her tent rustle, she spun her chair

around and faced the visitor. Amalia smiled at her as she entered the tent.

"I could hear you sighing from a mile away, child. What's on your mind?" Amalia took a seat on the edge of Annabel's bed.

Annabel frowned. "Andrew hasn't visited me in over a week. Do you think I've done something wrong?"

Amalia gave her a sad smile. "I don't think so, my little one. I'm not sure why he hasn't been around, but I do not think it was anything you did."

Annabel bit the inside of her cheek. "How can you be so sure? Why else would he stop visiting me?"

Amalia pressed her lips together in deep thought. Amalia always took great care in telling her the truth without hurting her feelings. "Honestly, there are a multitude of different reasons for his absence, each one as likely as the next." She reached out and grabbed one of Annabel's hands. "What I can tell you though, is that from the way he looked at you the last time he was here he wasn't offended in the slightest. It could just be that life got unexpectedly busy, and he hasn't had a chance to visit."

Annabel stared down at her hands, unsure of how to respond. Though she tried hard to prevent it, a sniffle broke past her defenses.

"Oh, my little one." Amalia wrapped her arms around the crying girl. "I know I am not your mother, but I care for you as if you were my own. My heart breaks seeing you this way." She pulled back and wiped the tears from Annabel's face. "'We must remember that everything happens for a reason, and it's all in the Lord's timing. Just wait and see what He has in store for you."

Annabelle wiped her tears and nodded. "You're right. It's just hard. For once, I felt like I was special to someone other than my family members."

Amalia pressed a kiss to her forehead. "You are so special, Annabel. Never question that."

The girl nodded and hugged Amalia. "Thank you. You may not be my mother, but you're the closest thing I've had to one in a long time." Annabel gave her a bright smile.

Tears began to collect in Amalia's eyes. "Don't you go making me blubber now. We've got a show to do. Are you ready?"

"I am now!" Annabel said as she finished putting her earrings on.

The women laughed as they exited the tent and threaded through the hub of the crowd. Annabel hoped and prayed that Andrew would be among them.

ANDREW MADE his way down to the breakfast table and greeted his parents. Today was the day. He would finally get to see her again. He could only wonder if she had missed him as much as he had missed her. His parents both returned his salutation before turning back to their papers and food.

After turning the page of his paper, his father glanced over the top at Andrew. "Your mother mentioned that you were going out today with some friends. I believe she said you're going to the cinema?"

Andrew was surprised at the question from his father whose attention had not left the newspaper he held in his hands. Quickly swallowing his food, he answered, "Yes, Father. I know for sure Charles and James will be there, but I'm not quite sure who else is joining us. And I'm not quite sure what they've chosen to see." Andrews half-lie seemed to appease his father as he asked no more questions.

After finishing his meal, he bade his parents goodbye and grabbed his hat and coat from the hall tree. Shutting the door behind him, Andrew took a deep breath. That was the first obstacle overcome without any difficulty. Now, he would just have to find a way to separate from his friends for a little while so he could visit his little mermaid. As he took off down the street, he couldn't help but feel like there was ice pouring into him from somewhere. It left an uncomfortable, almost tingling, sensation in his body. Glancing around, Andrew checked to see if he could spot anyone, but he could see neither person nor shadow lurking anywhere. It must just be his guilty conscience reprimanding him for his lie.

He found comfort in the coolness that permeated the air. It was cool enough that he was glad he grabbed his coat, but not cold enough that he was left shivering. It beat the unbearable summer heat. Not wanting to waste any time, Andrew took the shortcut to the subway station. Were his friends there already? Maybe they could leave sooner, and he could have more time with Annabel.

As he rounded the corner to the station, he spotted some familiar faces all huddled in a group.

"Ah! Here he is at last! We were beginning to wonder if you were just joshing me yesterday!" Charles laughed out, and the others joined in.

"Ha. Ha. Yes, it's real funny." Andrew rolled his eyes at their antics.

The subway car pulled into the station right at noon and they all piled inside. All situated in the back of the subway car, the others told him of their adventures over the past couple weeks. Andrew didn't mind passing the time in this way. He had missed his friends, so it was nice to learn what the last few weeks had held for them. It made the time go quicker too. Soon he would be on Coney Island and have his little mermaid by his side.

Stepping off the subway car, he took a deep breath of that familiar clean air. He was back at last. His friends made their way off as well, joining him right outside the station.

"Am I the only one that loves the air out here?" Andrew asked, inhaling deeply once more.

The others murmured in agreement.

Charles led them down the main road to the performance tent. Andrew's heart began to race. Would Annabel's heart flutter when she saw him? Had she missed him?

Andrew felt that familiar sensation again. The tingling that shot up his spine. Was there someone watching him? He looked over his shoulder, but the crowd was too big for anyone to stand out. It must just be his imagination. Andrew shook his head and focused on the tent in front of him. Any second he'd see *her* again.

They took their seats, Andrew asking to sit as close as possible to the front. As they announced the shows starting, he held his breath. This would be the moment of truth.

FIVE

Annabel waited in the wings for her turn to perform. She was running through her routine in her head when Amalia came back in from her performance. As Amalia walked toward her, Annabel wondered about the grin on the older woman's face.

"What has your grin so wide?" Annabelle asked with an eyebrow raised.

Amalia shrugged. "You'll just have to wait and see."

What? What kind of answer was that? Annabel frowned but did not press the woman further. She didn't have the time to anyway as they announced her set next.

Annabel spun herself around to look at Amalia. "Will you help me into my tank?"

She nodded.

Annabel wheeled herself onto the platform next to the top of the tank. Taking care not to rip her tail, she slid herself from the chair onto the floor. She waited there until Amalia had moved the chair, then she returned to help Annabel slip into the water.

That first plunge into the water was always shocking. Annabel reminded herself not to gasp as the coolness pressed against her skin. Hot water was a luxury they could not afford, so the best they could do was to let it sit out in the sunlight between shows. It didn't do much to help.

Annabel maneuvered herself to the top of the tank and grabbed the bars on each side. She needed to conserve her leg strength for the routine. Amalia closed the lid before giving Annabel a smile and a nod.

Annabel's heart thumped against her chest and her stomach began doing flips within her. She always had some nerves before the show, but they were never this bad. Amalia's wide smile had set Annabel on edge. What waited out there for her?

She held her breath as she heard Saoirse announced from the center of the ring. When the tank neared the entrance to the stage, Annabel took a deep breath before plunging down into the water. The lights from the ring shone through the water and lit up the sparkles on her tail. She swirled herself around, her arms moving in time with the music. She closed her eyes and let the water tell her how to move. Her legs cut through the water, swaying back and forth.

Her eyes opened, and she looked out at the crowd before her. Smiling, she waved at the little girls who stared at her in awe. A familiar set of hazel eyes met her green. Annabel's movements halted for a moment, but she quickly fell back into her routine so the audience wouldn't get restless.

Annabel's body moved on muscle memory because her mind focused on Andrew. *He came back.* Did this mean that he still wanted to be her friend and visit her? So many questions and thoughts ran through her mind that she hadn't even realized that her part was over, and she had been wheeled backstage. It wasn't until the lid was opened that she surfaced from her wonderings.

"Are you okay, my dear?" Her father asked as he held out a hand for her to take.

Annabel blinked and turned her gaze to the people above her. "I'm sorry?"

She reached out and took a hand from each of them. With relative ease, William and Amalia lifted Annabel from her glass tank. Her father held her upright while she was quickly wrapped up in a towel by Amalia. Once she was dried enough, they helped her to her chair and settled her in before they began their questioning.

"What's the matter, Annabel?" Her father knelt down in front of her and took both of her hands in his. His large hands encompassed her small ones, and she took comfort in the warmth of his thumbs rubbing her cool skin.

The girl took a minute to catch her breath. While the routine was relatively easy, it still involved a lot of moving and physical exertion. She brushed some of her wet hair behind her ear before giving her father a small smile.

"He was in the audience today," she finally answered.

William sighed, assuming that her answer would have something to do with the young lad. "Are you not happy that he's here? I thought you were excited to see him again?" He gave her hands a loving squeeze.

Annabel nodded her head. "I am. It's just…" She played with the towel wrapped around her. "What if he doesn't want to talk to me? He hasn't been here in a while, and it looks like he brought some of his friends. He most likely doesn't want to be seen with me." The girl's head hung low between her shoulders, her spine curled into an arch as she hunched over.

Annabel chanced a peek and saw her father look up at Amalia, his gaze soft and gentle. She patted him on the shoulder and waved for him to move.

"Oh, my dear one, I do not think you have anything to fear there. I've seen the way that boy looks at you. You have left him captivated since his very first visit. As for how he'll behave with his friends here, well, if he doesn't treat you right in front of his friends, then he doesn't deserve you." She wrapped her arms around the girl and squeezed. "Now, let's get you changed, then you can go out there and show that boy what he's been missing."

The two women giggled.

"Thank you, Amalia." Annabel said.

The woman nodded before grabbing the back of the wheelchair and heading out the back of the tent.

———

WILLIAM STOOD BEHIND, staring at the empty space the women had just abandoned. A sinking feeling filled his gut as he thought about his little girl and the young lad who had wormed his way into their lives. He loved that his daughter had found someone that made her happy, but there could be nothing but trouble ahead for them. His people would never let her join their world, and that thought broke his heart.

———

ANDREW FOLLOWED his friends around Coney Island as they enjoyed all the island had to offer. Every so often, they would stop and play at one of the stalls, and he watched as they spent their money on meaningless things. Andrew couldn't stop thinking about Annabel and her part of the show. What had happened while she was performing? Was she okay? Was she upset to see him here after being away for so long?

He slipped his right hand into his pocket. A cold sensation greeted his fingertips. Andrew smiled and delicately ran his thumb over the bracelet that resided there. He hoped the bracelet would make up for his absence the past few weeks. He knew he had no good excuse for his sudden disappearance, but he prayed her kind nature would prevail, and she'd forgive him. He wouldn't blame her if she didn't though. He still felt rather rotten about the whole thing.

Andrew had more pressing matters at hand though. How would he slip away from his friends long enough to see his little mermaid?

"Andrew!"

Andrew looked up at the sound of his name being called. "Hm? Sorry, I didn't catch that."

His friends all laughed.

"Where's your head been? You haven't been yourself since we've arrived." Charles bumped his shoulder into Andrew's.

Andrew protested. "What are you on about? I'm the way I always am!" He crossed his fingers hoping they'd accept his answer.

"Not a chance! Usually, you never shut up! You've been quiet since we met up at the station!"

Someone clapped Andrew on the back. "So, what's on your mind?"

Another voice chimed in, "Maybe it's a who? Or more specifically, a she?"

They all laughed and exchanged smirks. Andrew didn't like the looks on their faces.

And for good reason.

The next minute they all burst out into song, making merry at poor Andrew's expense. He grimaced and put a bit of distance between himself and the group.

Other guests threw angry glances at the group as the volume of their teasing grew loud enough to catch attention.

The band of jokers finished their song with a few guffaws before they turned their attention back to the attractions and stalls since Andrew had disappeared.

Andrew shook his head and rolled his eyes. He sometimes wondered why he was friends with them. Though, before he met Annabel, Andrew was often just like them. Who knew someone could change him so quickly?

How had this little mermaid become such an important person in his life after such a short amount of time? He had no answer for that question, and he decided he did not mind it one bit. He may not know all the answers, but he was happy she was a part of his life. He hoped she still wanted to be as well.

Someone bumped into his shoulder and knocked him from his thoughts. His friends were nowhere to be found. He wandered ahead for a bit trying to make them out in the crowd but still couldn't catch a glimpse of them.

"Perfect!" was the first thought that flew through his mind. He gave one last glance around him before making his way to the personal tents of the performers. His heart sped up, and his knees began to feel rather weak. Doubts clouded his mind the closer he made it to the tent. What if she didn't want to see him? What would he do if she no longer wanted to be in his company? His feet stopped right outside of Annabel's tent. He couldn't bring himself to make his presence known. His fear crescendoed and prevented him from moving forward. What would she do? What would her response be? Maybe he should do this a different day.

He had no time to change his mind as the flap was pulled back and left him face to face with William. Andrew jumped away at the sudden appearance of the ringleader.

"Excuse me, Mr. Thompson." Andrew tipped his hat at the older man.

William sighed before stepping through the entrance of the tent. "Hello, Andrew. What brings you here?" He crossed his arms, his eyes almost boring holes into Andrew's soul.

Andrew grabbed at the bracelet in his pocket and gave it a squeeze. The feeling of the cool metal against his fingertips provided the courage he needed to answer.

"I came to see Annabel. Is she here? I don't have a lot of time. I've only just got away from the friends I came with." Andrew rubbed the back of his neck and shifted his weight around.

He had no clue if William was angry with him for staying

away from his daughter for so long. Honestly, if Andrew were in William's shoes, he'd be angry with any young man who had hurt his daughter.

William crossed his arms and stared him down. "You've been away for quite a while, lad. Annabel's been in quite the state because of it."

Andrew's chest tightened, and his heart clenched within it. He never wanted to hurt Annabel. He'd stayed away to keep their friendship safe, but he may have ruined it anyway. His shoulders sagged.

"However, I assume you've had your reasons for being away. If I were to take a guess, I would say it has to do with your parents. Am I correct?"

Andrew nodded. "I'm not supposed to be here in the first place. My parents were getting suspicious. I needed to divert their attention for a bit of time before coming back." Andrew sighed. A chilly breeze blew through and made him shiver. "Believe me, I didn't want to stay away this long. I've quite missed this—" Andrew paused for a moment, thinking, "how does Annabel put it? Merry band of misfits?"

The leader chuckled. "Yes, I do believe that's what she calls us." He shook his head. "Silly girl. She really has missed you, lad."

"I've missed her too, sir," Andrew said honestly.

William nodded, pleased with the boy's answer. He pulled back the flap of the tent and gestured for Andrew to step inside. "I'm glad you came back. It's been too quiet without you around," he teased.

Andrew rolled his eyes before turning to face the tent entrance. He took a deep breath. He could do this. She missed him just as he missed her. There was nothing to worry about. His heart betrayed him though, as it thudded against his ribcage. He inhaled once more before stepping through the opening.

SIX

Annabel watched as her father left the tent, not thrilled by her lack of interest in the topic at hand. She'd already spoken to Amalia about Andrew earlier; she didn't wish to rehash the same conversation with her father. He could be too overprotective at times. Annabel was convinced he still saw her as a little girl who didn't know her own mind. But she did. Annabel knew there had to be a reason Andrew had kept away, one that didn't involve him being upset with her. She sighed, at least that's what Amalia had said.

The girl picked up her hairbrush and ran it through her hair, slowly working out any knots. Her chair sat at the mirror in her tent as her brush continued to glide through her hair. The red tones shone in lighting as the tool met no resistance. The movement it created in the water often left her with nasty knots she had to work out at the end of each show. One of her favorite things was when Amalia would pull up a chair behind Annabel's wheelchair and brush through her hair. Amalia's hands were always soft and gentle. Since Annabel had no memory of her mother, Annabel could only imagine this was what it must feel like to have a mother to care for you when you needed it. They may not be related by blood, but Amalia had been there for her almost her whole life and treated her like a daughter. Family wasn't only one's blood though, right? At least, that's what her father had taught her, and she had no qualms believing it. Besides, a chosen family was a much better family than blood in some cases.

She thought to the letters hidden in her wardrobe. She had received another one, and this one seemed angry and desperate. The handwriting on the outside had been the same, but the penmanship on the letter itself was completely different. Would his parents be willing to do something like this to drive her away? Annabel chided herself for such thoughts. She'd never met Andrew's parents, so it was unfair of her to assume so much about them.

She heard voices outside the tent. One she recognized as her father's, and the other one sounded an awful lot like Andrew's. Had Andrew finally come to visit? Would he explain why he'd been away for so long? Annabel smoothed out her skirt and looked over her outfit to make sure she looked fine before she intervened. As she wheeled herself to the entrance, a familiar figure stepped through.

"Hi there," Andrew said, voice soft and hesitant. His shoulders were hunched, and his head was bent a little lower than he usually held it.

Annabel could sense his nervousness and decided to put him out of his misery. A big smile spread across her face as she exclaimed, "Andrew! I'm so glad you're here. We've all missed you very much!"

A pink flush settled on Andrew's face, and a grin stretched across his face.

Annabel wheeled herself closer to Andrew. "Why have you been away so long?" She chose not to beat around the bush and just get straight to the point.

HER DIRECTNESS CAUGHT Andrew off guard. He knew she would ask him eventually, but he expected the conversation to start differently. He exhaled and ran a hand down his face. "I must apologize for the long absence. Things got a little tricky at home and prevented me from coming any sooner."

"Things got tricky at home?" Annabel's nose scrunched up. "I'm sorry. I don't understand."

"It's all right. I'll explain."

Annabel gestured to the chair by her vanity. "Please have a seat."

"Thank you very much." Andrew nodded and grabbed the chair, pulling it closer to where Annabel was sitting. He watched her fiddle with the fringe of the shawl that was wrapped around her shoulders. It was black with a beautiful floral pattern that really brought out the green in her eyes. She was still breathtakingly beautiful.

"So, you were saying about your parents?"

Andrew leaned forward, resting his elbows on his thighs. "My family has a certain position in New York society. My ancestors helped to build this country before it had even won its independence. Because of our status, my parents are very controlling about where I spend my time." Andrew gripped his chair with both hands. "I was never supposed to come here. They thought the attractions on this island were beneath us. They still do."

Annabel looked as though she wanted to interject, but she bit her lip and let Andrew continue.

"They've been so suspicious the last month or so that I couldn't risk coming out here to see you and having them find out about our secret." Andrew knew that honesty was the best approach to the situation. Though he didn't want to hurt Annabel's feelings, he thought the situation warranted the truth. She deserved nothing less. "They think I've been behaving strangely lately so they've been keeping a close eye on me. I couldn't risk coming back here while they were still watching me."

Annabel frowned. "What would they do if they caught you coming here?"

Andrew shook his head. "I don't know, and I don't want to risk it. You have all become too important to me to risk losing." He leaned forward and took her small hands in his larger ones. He marveled at how soft they were despite her spending so much time submerged in water. "Your group has become more of a family to me than my parents have ever been. Being away for these past weeks was the hardest thing I've ever done in my life."

His THUMBS TRACED the back of her hands. Annabel smiled at the act of affection. Her soul soared at his confession. She'd spent so long worrying about what she had done to drive him away, but all along he'd been protecting her. This man had captured her heart in a completely unexpected way.

She tilted forward in her chair, the wheels groaning at the shift in her weight. Her lips met his cheek in a gentle kiss.

As she pulled back, she noticed the flush back on his face. This time though, she could feel the heat of her own blush as well.

"Thank you, Andrew. For explaining and protecting us."

Andrew sat there, unmoving, his jaw slack. Slowly, he reached his hand up to the place where she had kissed, a boyish grin overtaking his features. "You're welcome."

Annabel giggled at his reaction.

The tent flap was thrown open, and Levi ran in. He panted as he tried to get his words out, chest heaving with exertion. "Andrew...friends...looking for...him."

Andrew's eyes widened. "I must go before they find me

here. I don't know what they would do if they did. I don't want to take the chance."

Andrew stood up and made his way toward the exit, but when he reached it, he stopped. Whipping around, he marched right back over to Annabel and pulled the bracelet from his pocket. He placed it in her hand. "I bought this for you, my little mermaid," he said, then quickly pecked her lips before speeding out of the tent.

Annabel sat there, her eyes large. This time, she was the one who lifted her fingers to where he had kissed. And like him, she smiled.

———

ANDREW RAN from the tent as fast as he could. What had possessed him to kiss her like that? What if she found it too forward and was angry with him?

Sudden movement to his left caught his attention. He thought he saw someone ducking around the side of the tent.

"Hello? Is someone there?" Andrew asked. His stomach twisted. What if one of his friends had seen him? He tiptoed to the edge of the tent and peered around the side. There was no one there.

Odd. Had he imagined the whole thing? But this wasn't the first time it had happened that day. The thought made him uneasy. He weaved through the tents and stepped back into the crowded Main Street of the island.

"Andrew!"

He turned around at the sound of his name. The group of friends he had separated from stood before him.

"Where did you go, man?" They surrounded him, one patting him on his shoulder.

Andrew found that he had not missed his friends very much. Younger Andrew would have been shocked to discover this, but it was the unfortunate truth. They were so carefree and pursued no real purpose in life. He had once been like that as well, but after spending time with the crew of Thompson's Traveling Wonders, he had a new outlook on life. He'd also fallen in love with the beautiful mermaid who was the heart of the troupe. They supported and cared for each other. Andrew was still envious of all the time they spent together, whether it was playing games or gathering together to study the Bible. He wanted it all.

"You all right?" Charles' voice ripped him from his thoughts.

"I'm sorry?" Andrew asked.

The group of young men exchanged concerned looks.

One of them piped up, "Let's head back. I think Andrew's had too much fun today."

Andrew was ready to head home, but it had nothing to do with having had too much fun. They all followed the crowd as they made their way to the station. He couldn't be bothered to join in the conversations his friends were having. New cars, new clothing, the cinema. Andrew was disenchanted with it all. More than once, he had considered giving it all up.

He settled himself into his subway seat, unwilling to go back to the practically empty house. A man clothed entirely in black stepped onto the car right before it started to move. The man sat down on the seat across from Andrew. He pulled a newspaper from his coat pocket and buried his face in it.

Andrew turned his attention away from the man. After a few moments though, he felt as though he was being watched, but when he looked around, no one was focused on him. He went back to gazing at the floor of the subway car, his nerves alight.

The same sensation creeped upon him yet again. This time, he kept his head low but flicked his gaze up to the people that were around him. It was quick, but Andrew made eye contact with the man in black, who quickly went back to the paper. *Could he really be watching me?*

As soon as the subway car pulled into the station, Andrew said goodbye to his friends and took off down the street. Who was that man on the train, and why was the man watching him? He headed in the direction of Central Park. The streets were full of families taking an evening stroll together. It was one of the few things his family used to do together when he was younger, but Andrew assumed it was more to keep up appearances than to spend time together as a family.

Andrew looked at his reflection in a shop window he walked by only to see the man in black following a short distance behind him. His stomach dropped. Was he being followed now? He took a sudden right at the next street, trying to subtly check if the man made the turn too. He did. Fear coursed through Andrew's veins, making it harder for him to breathe. He needed to get home. If this man was smart, he wouldn't set foot on the property. Andrew just had to make it home first. He took the next left and cut through an alleyway between the buildings to shave off some time. He tried to keep his pace as natural as possible so he wouldn't tip the man off, but he made it his mission to get home in a timely manner.

At the sight of the large townhouse, Andrew heaved out a sigh. He burst through the door and slammed it behind him. His chest heaved as he sank to the floor, his limbs finally giving out on him. Roger, their butler, entered the room a few minutes later.

"Sir, are you quite all right?" he asked. The contempt on his face was clear to Andrew, but he chose to ignore it.

Andrew nodded, still trying to catch his breath. "I think I'll head upstairs now."

"Shall I have a tray sent up to your room?"

Andrew was grateful for the older man in moments like this. "Yes, Roger. Thank you."

Roger nodded and walked out of the room, leaving Andrew on his own once more. He pushed himself up off the ground and trudged up the stairs to his bedroom. He pressed against his door as he opened it, then stepped into the room. As Andrew got ready for bed, many thoughts chased each other through his mind.

What exactly had happened today? He had started out nervous about seeing Annabel again, and when they were reunited, he'd been filled with such joy. That joy didn't last though under the weight of the terror he had felt when he had realized the man was following him. Who was this man clothed in all black? More importantly, why was he following Andrew?

Andrew was running on muscle-memory now. He ate his meal but couldn't have told anyone what it was had he been asked. He slipped into his nightwear and crawled into bed.

He fell into an uneasy sleep, contemplating all of the possibilities of what exactly was happening in his life. He hoped that, come morning, he might have at least a few answers.

SEVEN

A few days later, Andrew walked down the stairs and plopped himself at the breakfast table. He knew something was going on when he noticed both of his parents there waiting for him.

"Mother. Father," he greeted as he placed his napkin in his lap.

Andrew's mother smiled at him. "Andrew, dear, your father and I have something we wish to discuss with you."

His heart clenched at her words. What could they possibly want to talk to him about? He gripped his knees but tried to keep his expression neutral. "Oh? What about?" The question came out much shakier than he had hoped for.

Andrew's father clasped his hands together. "We have some very important guests coming over tonight. I expect you to be here and on your best behavior."

His mother put her hand on his father's arm. "These aren't just any guests, darling. They're members of the Porter family. They hold an important place in society."

Andrew could have sworn he saw his mother give him a stern look at those words. What was that supposed to mean?

"They have a daughter that's about your age," she continued, "and we have decided to bring our families together with your union to their daughter Valerie."

Andrew's fork clanked against his plate as he pushed his chair back. "What?" Fury flared deep within his chest. How dare they try to control his life in this way! Who would ever want to be married off to someone they didn't know? Especially when his heart had already been stolen by another. He took a deep breath before standing up and addressing his parents.

"I'm sorry, but I cannot marry a woman I've never met before," he snapped.

His father also pushed up from the table. "How dare you speak to your mother and me like that! We are your parents, and you will show some respect." His face was turning red at an alarming rate. Andrew worried his father's head would explode any second.

"I'm not something you can just sell off. What if I have someone I'm already in love with?"

Both his parents scowled, and his father clenched his fists so tight the skin began to turn white. "You will do as I say, or so help me, you will live to regret it."

Andrew had never seen his father so angry, and the sight of it terrified him to the very core. The weight of his parents' demeanors pushed him back into his chair. They were dead serious about this, and Andrew knew that nothing was going to change their minds. He would have to meet Valerie tonight. He would assuage his parents' wrath by doing what they wanted for now, but he refused to let them come between him and the girl he loved. When it came down to it, he would fight for her. He would give up everything for Annabel. Nothing his parents did would stop him. That was a promise. A vow for his little mermaid.

Roger had laid out Andrew's outfit for the evening at his mother's request. His heart and mind struggled with the temptation to become bitter and filled with hatred for his parents. Would he ever be allowed to lead his own life without them breathing down his neck and trying to control as many aspects of it as they could? He threw on the outfit, stopping just to make sure his mother would have nothing to nitpick when it came to his appearance. This night would be miserable enough as it was. He didn't need to add any more fuel to the fire of his current suffering. Andrew placed his hand on the doorknob on his bedroom door and inhaled deeply before stepping out and closing the door behind him. He heard voices floating up from the foyer below. They were already here, so it was time for Andrew to play the part his parents expected of him. All he could do was pray he made his performance convincing enough for them to believe. Too bad he wasn't able to ask any of the troupe for some pointers on how to sell this to everyone tonight.

He took his time walking down the stairs. Everyone was waiting for him below when he entered the foyer.

"Andrew! There you are. We were concerned you would make us late to sit down for dinner. Let's head in, and we can eat." His mother threw him a disapproving look before she followed behind her guests.

The placement of the seats was not lost on Andrew. He noticed he and Valerie had been placed next to each other where their parents no doubt hoped the two would talk and get on well. Andrew hated to disappoint them. Well, not completely.

Once seated at the table, the staff came in and served the first course while both sets of parents chatted. Andrew would have preferred to ignore the girl at his side. He'd rather not deal with her at the current moment.

The two of them exchanged polite talk until she leaned over and whispered, "Isn't this just the bee's knees? I've been looking forward to this meeting all day. I think it's a smart match."

It took all of Andrew's willpower not to scoff or make some snide remark. "My parents think so," was all he replied.

Her brow furrowed at his response. "Do you not think so, Andy?"

"I'd rather not answer." He knew his words were harsh, but he did not want to give her false hope. Nor did he care for the nickname.

After that, dinner was a quiet affair. It wasn't until their guests were getting ready to leave that they really spoke again. Valerie waited until their parents were out of hearing distance to question Andrew. "What's her name?"

The inquiry startled him. "What's whose name?"

She sighed. "The girl's name. I'm guessing that is the reason you do not want to marry me. There must be someone else."

Andrew wanted to roll his eyes. Who did this woman think she was? He wondered if she was aware of how conceited she sounded. He guessed not.

"I don't know what you're talking about."

She scoffed. "Tell it to Sweeney. I know there has to be someone else."

"Whether there's a girl or not is none of your concern. I'll bid you good evening." He kissed the back of her hand before escorting her to their parents.

As soon as their guests were out the door, Andrew took off for his room without sparing his parents a single glance.

EIGHT

The next few days didn't get any better for Andrew. He had no idea what made his parents decide to push so hard, but at this point, he was so tired of seeing Valerie. She wasn't completely horrible, but being forced to spend time with someone can greatly affect any relationship.

Today, he had managed to wiggle out of spending any time with Valerie. He was up, dressed, and at the subway stop for the first trip to Coney Island.

The view from the station to the island never got old to Andrew. He loved the feeling of the air getting cooler as the distance to his favorite place lessened. The crispness against his skin made him feel refreshed and energized. The sting in his lungs from the temperature was a welcome change from the atmosphere back home. Coney Island made him feel like a new man every time he visited. He wished he could keep feeling like that man when he went home. He craved that person when he was surrounded by his friends and family, but he worried about what they would think of him. Would they push him away?

The more time that passed since Andrew's first visit to

Coney, the more he found himself not caring what they would think of him. His parents were trying to force him into a marriage he had no interest in. His desire to spend time with his friends had lessened. A part of him considered packing up and joining Annabel's family.

The announcement of their arrival rang out through the car from the man at the front. Andrew gathered his coat and hat before making his way out the door. The main pathway through the island was fairly clear today so the foot traffic was easy enough to wade through. The wet dirt squelched beneath his shoes as he headed for the performance tent. When he walked inside, the stands were empty, and some of the performers were cleaning up the stage. They smiled and waved when they saw Andrew standing at the entrance of the tent. He smiled and waved back. He was always welcomed here, and it was something Andrew never wanted to take for granted. A warm expression and a greeting were always waiting for him among this troupe. Once again, he longed to have a family like this one. For his parents to actually care about him like this group did.

Andrew slipped out of the tent and headed for Annabel's. Along the way, he met William.

"Andrew, my boy! It's so good to see you!" William shook his hand.

A grin overtook his face. "William, you too! I hope everyone is well."

The man nodded. "Annabel will be so happy to see you. She's grown quite attached."

"I've grown quite attached to her as well." Andrew blushed but told the truth.

William laid a hand on his shoulder. "I can tell. You're a good man, and I know that you'd take care of her." A sigh escaped his lips. "I just worry about her. People will talk, and they will be unkind. I don't know if she could handle it. She's a very kind girl with a soft heart."

Andrew's stomach dropped at the man's words. He couldn't deny the truth of what the man said, no matter how much he wished he could. The wind blew past them, but the coldness that settled against Andrew's skin couldn't be blamed on the wind. Could he really put Annabel through that? If he felt as much for her as he thought, would he want to subject her to that kind of treatment for the rest of her life? So many questions swirled around his head. A sharp pain was starting to form between his eyes.

As if sensing his distress, William interjected, "I'm not saying she couldn't, and I'm not telling you not to pursue her. It's not really for me to decide anyway. She knows her own mind, and it'll be the rest of her life, not mine. I'm going to let her make that decision for herself. Go talk to her." William patted Andrew's shoulder before walking away.

Andrew's feet carried him to the front of Annabel's tent. Was he really ready to have this conversation with her? With everything that was going on with Valerie, he wanted—no needed—to know if Annabel truly felt the same way he did. Then he would determine what to do from there.

"Annabel? Can I come in?" Andrew called through the flap of the tent.

"Andrew? Is that you?" came her reply.

"It is."

"Come in!"

Andrew took a deep breath before stepping through the tent opening.

His heart always sped up the first moment he saw her. Her hair was still a beautiful vibrant red, and her green eyes glimmered in the lighting of the tent. She was a vision he would never tire of seeing.

"Andrew?" Annabel wheeled herself over to where he stood, but he hadn't noticed it in his daze.

"Hi," was all he managed to get out.

She giggled and shook her head. A small smile graced her

face, and Andrew was proud that he was the cause of it. He hoped he could continue to make her smile for the foreseeable future.

"Did you need something? Or did you just come to visit?" she asked.

"I, uh, I came to talk to you about something," he stuttered.

Her eyebrows raised, and she tilted her head. "Oh? What about?"

Andrew shifted his weight from foot to foot as he fiddled with the top hat in his hands. "Um…"

Annabel gestured to the chair near her vanity. "Would you like to sit?"

He nodded and made for the chair, but not without tripping on his own feet. "Sorry. I'm not usually this clumsy."

She shook her head. "No need to apologize. Are you all right, though?"

He nodded again then sat down. He took a few deep breaths, trying to steady his nerves.

────────

HIS BEHAVIOR MADE ANNABEL NERVOUS. She'd never seen him act like this. It must be something serious. Was he going to stop coming to visit her? Had something happened at his home? She felt bombarded by all the questions that just kept piling up in her thoughts.

"Annabel, I know I haven't been visiting Coney Island for long, but you've all become so important to me. I honestly don't know what I'd do without you all now," Andrew paused, his breath shaky as he exhaled. "I don't know what I'd do without *you*. You're always on my mind, and I want to be here with you all the time."

Annabel's breath hitched. He wanted to be with her? Was he implying what she thought he was? She didn't want to get her hopes up, but butterflies erupted in her stomach as she waited for him to continue.

"I'm so in love with you, Annabel Thompson. I know we've only known each other some months now, but I honestly cannot imagine my life without you in it. I look forward to seeing your eyes light up when you see me, your laughter when you find something funny, or the way you bite your lip when you're in deep thought. I love it all." He leaned forward and took her hands in his. "I adore your unfailing kindness towards anyone you meet. You have taught me so much about what you believe, not just through your words, but through your actions as well."

Tears welled up in Annabel's eyes. No one outside of her family had ever spoken to her like this. She had no idea she had this effect on anyone. Her heart warmed at his words, and the tears spilled over.

Andrew's eyes grew wide. He reached out and wiped them from her cheeks. "I'm so sorry, Annabel. I didn't mean to make you cry."

She sputtered out a laugh. "It's just because I'm so happy and touched. I've never had anyone outside my family say such lovely things to me."

His hands cradled her face. His touch was soft as his thumb rubbed her cheek. She closed her eyes and sighed happily. Bringing her hands up, she placed hers over his and squeezed. He leaned forward and pressed his lips to hers.

The kiss was brief but enough to convey what they both felt. As Annabel pulled back, a blush and a smile spread across her face. But it faded quickly when she noticed the expression on Andrew's face.

Annabel hesitated, then whispered, "Is something wrong?"

Andrew ran his fingers through his hair. "Yes. I love you, and nothing would make me happier than spending the rest of my life with you. However, there's something important we have to talk about first."

The questions came back to Annabel with a vengeance. What did they need to talk—oh, her legs. Of course. How could she be so stupid?

"Alight."

He gave her a half-smile. "As you know, my family is one of the more prominent ones of the area, and that brings a lot of attention."

Annabel nodded. She'd figured as much. Did he not want to be seen with her? Would he be embarrassed to be seen with her in public? Was he going to ask her to keep their relationship a secret? Her head began to swim, but the feeling of Andrew squeezing her hands brought her back to the surface.

"Before I ask to court you, I just need to make sure you understand what being with me would entail, Annabel. It won't be easy." He bit his lip as he looked at her. "People will make comments. They'll say mean things. They'll try to do what they can to drive us apart."

Annabel's heart warmed at his thoughtfulness and care for her. He wasn't worried about his reputation. He was worried about *her*. What had she done for such a kind-hearted soul to be sent her way?

"I don't want to be selfish and ask you to be mine without letting you know what future we face. I don't want you to get hurt, but it's inevitable given the world I come from. If you don't want to have to face all that and put yourself in the position to be treated that way, I understand." A lone tear made its way down his pale cheek as he stared at their joined hands.

Annabel pulled one of hers from his and wiped the tear for him as he had done for her. "Oh, Andrew. I've dealt with mean comments, judgmental glances, and harsh treatment for most of my life already. Enduring those things would be worth it to be able to be with you." She smiled and held the side of his face in her hand. "You are one of the kindest men I have ever met in my life. I would be honored to be courted by you, Andrew. There's nothing I want more."

An incredulous laugh escaped Andrew's lips. The smile on his face was infectious as he threw his arms around her and lifted her out of her chair. She couldn't help but laugh and squeal as he spun her around and placed a soft kiss against her lips again.

William rushed into the tent, alerted by his daughter's squeal.

"Is everything okay, little one?"

Annabel looked up at her father. She was in Andrew's arms, wide smiles stretched across both her and Andrew's faces. Andrew's hands supported her weight, and her arms were thrown around his neck.

"So, I take it you said yes," William remarked, a small grin on his own face. He was happy for his daughter, yet his heart ached at the trouble he knew was still to come. The likelihood of his daughter getting hurt was something he wished he didn't have to think about. All he could do now was support them and do whatever he could to keep his little girl from suffering too much.

NINE

Andrew left Annabel's tent with a spring in his step. She said yes! No words could describe the joy he felt in that moment. It filled him up and left him ready to explode with suppressed emotions. It all popped like a balloon when he saw someone running away from the tents toward the trolley. He didn't get a good look at the man's face, but the clothing was familiar enough for him to know it was the same man who had followed him the other day.

Andrew took off as fast as he could after him but didn't make it to the subway station in time. All Andrew wanted to know is who the man was and why he'd been followed. He didn't know, but he intended to find out.

After catching his breath, he went back to find William. The chill of the sea air felt nice against Andrew's flushed skin after the running he had done. The multicolored tents stood out against the backdrop of the blue sky, and posters hung everywhere, displaying the different performers of the troupe. He stopped at the one that showcased his beautiful mermaid. The poster represented her well. He loved how the artist had managed to capture her beauty in such detail.

"Andrew? What are you doing back here? I thought you had left," a familiar voice said to his left.

Andrew was startled out of his reverie. "William! I had, but something happened, and I had to come back to tell you. Someone was following me! I tried to watch him but he disappeared at the station."

"Hm, it seems someone has hired him to spy on you." William narrowed his eyes and scratched his cheek.

"Spy on me?" Andrew questioned with furrowed brows.

"Yes. My guess is that the man is a private detective sent to see what you've been up to. Can you think of anyone who would be willing to go to such lengths to see where you've been going?"

Andrew's face paled at the inquiry. He could, and it meant trouble. Lots of it, in fact. Was what he had with Annabel going to end before it could even start? He shook the thought from his mind. No. He'd fight when the time came for it. His parents had gone too far in their attempts to control his life. And Andrew was having no more of it.

———

ANDREW GOT off the subway and took off toward his home. He didn't expect to be stopped by someone he knew along the way.

"Andy!"

He scowled. He hated that nickname, and there was only one person who called him that. He looked to his left and spotted her standing next to the exit. "Valerie, fancy meeting you here." Sarcasm laced his words.

"Dry up, Andrew. I was looking for you. It's urgent." She grabbed his wrist and pulled him off to the side. "There's trouble waiting for you at home. Your parents are furious." She looked around quickly before continuing. "I went to visit you but heard someone telling them about you and a crippled girl in a wheelchair. Something about you being caught kissing her in her own tent. I think it's absolutely ludicrous. Why would someone make up such a horrid lie about you?" She fixed him with a passive look, but he could see her anticipation at his answer.

Andrew grit his teeth before taking a deep breath to calm himself. He looked towards the entrance of the station before answering, "It's not a lie, and her name is Annabel."

Valerie took a step back. "But you're engaged to me, for crying out loud! We're to be married within a year."

His head whipped around to face her. "What?"

She welled up, her eyes glassy and voice wobbly as she spoke. "Our parents settled this when we were there last. Did you not hear it?"

Andrew shook his head. "No. I didn't." His fists clenched at his sides. How dare they do this to him!

"They're going to be disappointed with the outcome of this," he muttered to himself.

Valerie took a step closer. "What do you mean by that?"

He sighed and ran a hand down his face. "I can't marry you, Valerie. I'm sorry. You're a nice girl, but you're not the one for me."

Her face went red. She opened her mouth but closed it again. She worried her bottom lip before asking, "There's no changing your mind on this?"

He shook his head. "I'm so incredibly in love with her."

Valerie closed her eyes for a moment and wiped away the few tears that had escaped. "Okay, then I guess I'll just have to help you."

Andrew furrowed his brows. "I'm sorry?"

"I'll just have to help you. I really like you, Andrew, and I want you to be happy. If that means helping you be with the woman you love, then I'll do it."

She gave him a small smile. It was a watery one, but a smile nonetheless.

Looking around for any prying eyes and finding none, Andrew gave her a brief hug. "Thank you so much. I can't tell you how much this means to me."

She wrapped her arms around him and squeezed him. "Alight. Let's go soothe your parents' fury."

"And how do you intend to do that?" He raised an eyebrow.

She started walking away but turned back to say, "By telling them that you've come to your senses, and your infidelity ends here."

"Wait, what? How does that help me?" He took long strides to catch up with her.

She rolled her eyes and didn't bother to stop. "We play the fake fiancé angle. They think you're still with me, and we just have to get creative on how to get you and whatever her name is together."

"Annabel. Her name is Annabel."

Valerie waved her hand, "Yes, yes, Annabel. We'll have to make this convincing, and it'll take some planning, but I think we can pull it off."

Andrew wasn't as sold on this plan as she was, but he didn't really have much of a choice.

"Trust me, Andy. This will work."

He tried not to be irritated at the name. She was helping him. He needed to keep her on his side, and this was a small price to pay for it.

The walk was relatively silent the rest of the way. Nerves set in as soon as his house came into view. It was time to put on a show, one he hoped was as believable as the one William's troupe put on.

───────

ANDREW HELD the front door open for Valerie to step through and closed it behind them. The house was utterly silent. It sent a chill down Andrew's spine. He could already tell a storm was brewing, and he was about to get caught in it.

Valerie wrapped her arm around his. He looked at her from the corner of his eye.

"We have to make this convincing," she whispered.

Andrew hated it, but he knew she was right. He wanted it to be Annabel holding his arm as he escorted her, but his parents most likely wouldn't even let her in the front door. He hated how prejudiced they could be.

His parents came around the corner, both of their expressions tight.

"Mr. and Mrs. Grayson." Valerie beamed at both of them. "It's good to see you again."

His mother smiled back at her. "Valerie, dear, it's so good to see you. We were concerned when Roger said you had left shortly after you arrived."

She nodded. "Sorry about that. I heard what had gone on and went to find Andrew myself." She smiled up at him. "We've talked about it and sorted everything out. Now he's on the trolley. All is forgiven, and his infidelity ends today. Isn't that right, Andy?"

He looked down at her and plastered a small smile on his face. "Yes." He faced his parents. "She's been very kind and forgiving. I'm done visiting the island and the girl there. I know that you guys know about her. There's no point in me hiding it now." He hung his head low, hoping it looked like he was disappointed in himself.

His parents eyed him for a moment; he guessed they were gauging the sincerity of his apology.

"Very well. Valerie, will you go on ahead to the dining room? We have dinner laid out there. I'm sure there's plenty for you to have some as well," his mother said.

Valerie looked at him, and he nodded to her. His parents weren't going to let this go that easily. She walked through the entryway toward the dining room.

Andrew watched as his parents drew closer to him. He could tell by their expressions that this would be a very uncomfortable conversation. There was nothing he could do to avoid it at this point. Unless he faked fainting. That might work. He'd only be delaying the inevitable though. It was better to get it out of the way now than have to continue dreading it. He sighed and waited for his parents to begin their interrogation.

"Andrew Thomas Grayson, what on earth were you thinking? Gallivanting around with some freak show cripple." His mother rubbed her temples. "I thought we raised you better than that. What if someone else had seen you? What would happen to your reputation? To our family's reputation? Don't you care about us at all?"

It took every ounce of self-control Andrew had not to give the answer he really wanted to. How he would love to just blurt out what he thought of them and their reputation. It didn't matter to him anymore. He had someone who loved him when he was just himself. Just Andrew. But he needed to stick to Valerie's plan.

"I'm sorry, Mother. I don't know what I was thinking. It just happened," he lied.

His father crossed his arms and stepped forward. "You've been spending quite a bit of time on that island. I don't think you're telling us the truth."

Andrew wanted to growl and stomp upstairs, but that would be counterproductive. Instead, he took a deep breath. "She was pretty and nice to me. They all were nice to me. I was drawn to that, I guess."

His mother scoffed. "And they were just drawn to your money. Honestly, Andrew, I've told you since you were young that people like that are only out to trick you out of every penny you have." She stepped closer to him and put her hand on his shoulder. "I'm just looking out for you, son. I don't want you to get hurt. You're important to me."

He wanted to laugh. Important to her? Ha. That was tragically laughable. She only cared about what would happen if word got out that her son was seen kissing a performer at the freak show. He really hated that term. He had used it himself, but that was before he got to know the people there. Before he got to know Annabel. She wasn't a freak. She was a beautiful woman with feelings, a heart, a soul. The only thing that made her different was that she had been born with conjoined legs. That didn't make her any less beautiful to him. Why should it?

"Well, you don't have to worry anymore. Valerie and I have talked it out. If you'll excuse me, I'm hungry, and my future wife is waiting for me."

He stalked in the same direction Valerie had gone.

"Come back here, young man. Your mother and I aren't finished talking to you!" His father's voice echoed down the hallway. Andrew ignored it and kept walking. They would have to get used to him not doing everything they said. Whether they liked it or not, he was going to start forming his own path. This was his life, and he was going to live it in the way he wanted. Their prejudice had no room in his world. It was no longer a part of him, and it wouldn't be again.

Valerie tilted her head at him as he entered the room. "That sounded lively."

Andrew rolled his eyes. He took a seat beside her. "Are you sure this plan will work?" He couldn't help the bit of doubt he felt about her plan, but he also couldn't deny that it was better than any plan he could have come up with. Hers had a better chance of succeeding. He just couldn't help but feel that this was betraying Annabel in some way. He didn't want to ruin what he had with her in his attempt to save it. He could only pray everything would work out.

TEN

Annabel leaned down and slipped the bottom part of her fins onto her feet. She loved the feel and look of the sheer purple material that created the fin effect. She also loved the way the sparkly material of the tail caught the light when she was spinning in the water tank. Purple had been her favorite color for as long as she could remember. Part of her wondered if it was because the blanket her mother had made her as a baby was purple. It had been a way for her to connect with her mom even though her mother was gone.

She had shimmied the fabric up to her thighs at the edge of the chair when Amalia came in with a big smile on her face.

"Hey there! You need some help?"

Annabel nodded, grateful for the extra set of hands. She could manage the tail on her own, but it was rather difficult. Having help made the process so much smoother. She placed her hands on Amalia's shoulders and pushed herself up. The woman quickly hiked up the tail the rest of the way and lowered Annabel back into her chair.

"I love this tail. It makes me feel like a real mermaid." Annabel ran her hand over the fabric.

Amalia laughed. "You are a real mermaid. At least to me you are. Never let anyone convince you otherwise, okay?"

Annabel grinned. "Okay."

"Five minutes before you're needed backstage." Amalia headed towards the tent opening.

"Amalia!" Annabel called out.

The woman turned back around. "Yes?"

"Andrew calls me his little mermaid."

Amalia shook her head and giggled. "He's quite smitten with you, that young man. I'm glad he finally got the courage to ask to court you. You're good for each other."

Annabel blushed. "You really think so?"

The older woman nodded. "He adores you, and I know he'll treat you well." She smirked. "If he doesn't, we'll either feed him to Leo the Lion, or we'll make him one of the performing animals."

Both women burst into fits of laughter.

William walked into the tent, confused as to why the two were laughing so hard. "What's going on in here?"

Annabel bit her lip as she looked at her father but started laughing again when she made eye contact with Amalia.

Amalia merely smiled at William before answering, "Nothing, just a joke between women. You wouldn't understand."

His daughter nodded.

"I hope it's not about me then," he said as he scratched the back of his head.

"Oh no, Father! Not at all." She gave him a warm grin and wheeled herself to him. "You don't have to worry about that."

He let out a deep breath.

"We'd tell you if it was about you."

His jaw dropped as he looked at his beautiful daughter. The women started laughing again.

He pouted. "You guys are teaming up against me. It isn't fair."

Annabel and Amalia looked at each other before leaning in and each kissing a cheek.

"Chin up, William. You've got a show to run!" Amalia yelled back to him as she ran out of the tent.

He shook his head and chuckled.

"You should tell her, Father," Annabel said from beside him.

William looked down at her. "Tell her what?"

She rolled her eyes. "You know what. Tell her how you feel about her."

Red tinted her father's face, and he spluttered.

Annabel laughed and patted his arm. "It's just something to think about. I'd be fine with it, you know."

She wheeled herself out of the tent and off toward the performance area.

William ran a hand through his hair, shaking his head. "She's so much like her mother." He sighed. "These women are going to be the death of me." He followed behind his daughter to get ready for the next set of performances.

HE FOUND Amalia and Annabel huddled together once again. This time, neither of them looked happy and carefree. Tears were collecting in his daughter's eyes, a sight that always made his insides twist and his heart hurt. He rushed to her side.

"Darling! What's the matter?" He kneeled down beside her and held her face in his big hands.

Annabel just shook her head; she couldn't bring herself to answer his question.

He looked up at Amalia, hoping for some explanation for his daughter's behavior. Her brows were furrowed, and the corners of her lips were pulled down.

"It's Andrew." She pointed her chin toward the flap of the stage entrance. "Look out there."

William stood up and strode toward the stage. Peeking out at the audience, his eyes landed on the boy they were talking about. A woman sat with her own arm around Andrew's arm. He scanned the boy's face, looking for any sign of what he was feeling. One corner of Andrew's lips were turned down, and his brows were slightly furrowed. William wondered just what was going on. He had no doubt that Andrew was absolutely in love with his daughter as adoration radiated from him anytime he looked at her. There was no trace of that on his face as he sat next to this girl. Something deeper was happening, and though William didn't know what, he would certainly find out. He wasn't going to let his daughter hurt any more than she already was so he would get to the bottom of this and have a word with the boy.

He moved back to Annabel's side and wrapped his arms around her small frame.

"It's fine, my dear. I will find out what is going on, and I will fix this. Don't you worry your pretty little fins, all right?" He ran his fingers through her hair and rubbed her back soothingly.

She giggled against his chest, making him smile. He missed the days where she'd turned to him with all her troubles, and he especially missed that he had usually been able to solve them with just a hug and a kiss to the forehead. He hoped this situation could be resolved just as easily.

But that all depended on Andrew.

ANDREW GUIDED Valerie off the subway car and onto the platform at Coney Island. His heart soared at the thought of getting to see Annabel after all the trouble going on at home, but he knew this trip wouldn't be easy. Valerie had been trying way too hard to sell this relationship, and he was doing his best to be patient. He needed this ploy to work, or he wouldn't be able to see Annabel again until he escaped from his parents' clutches. With the way they'd been hovering every second of the day, he now believed they'd find a way to keep him locked up if they felt it necessary. He didn't want to add that to his list of obstacles to overcome. At least Valerie had suggested this visit so they really couldn't complain about it. He thanked her for that. He questioned her motivation, but she seemed to really want to help him so he would just take her at her word.

They wandered down the main walkway of the island, stopping every so often for Valerie to look at one of the stalls along the way. Andrew tapped his foot and crossed his arms as he stood there. What was so interesting about what they sold? They had come to see the show, not stop and look at everything being sold. Well, "everything" was an exaggeration, but it sure felt like she was stopping to look at everything to him. She bought a little trinket and turned to him.

"This is so adorable. I just had to get it." She held up the little figure for him to see.

Andrew rolled his eyes. "Yes, it looks nice. Can we move on? I don't want to miss the show." He spun around and started walking toward the main tent.

Valerie huffed but followed behind him. She stumbled a bit on the gravel pathway, not used to walking on such terrain with her heels.

"Don't, Andrew!" she called up to him.

He slowed with a sigh. "Hurry. The show starts in a couple of minutes."

They stepped through the entrance of the tent, and Andrew led them to his favorite seat.

"We get the best view here."

"I see." Valerie scooted closer and wrapped her arms around his right bicep.

He turned his head to look at her. "What are you doing?" His gaze moved down to where their arms were linked.

She looked back at him and raised an eyebrow. Tilting her head, she answered, "This place gives me the heebie-jeebies. And, if anyone we know is here, we want them to think we're on a date. Not that you've dragged me along to see your other woman."

Andrew desperately desired to tell her that she was technically the other woman but decided it wasn't worth the effort. He had more important things to think about, like how he was going to explain this to Annabel without having William come after him. Or Amalia for that matter. That woman could be downright scary when she wanted to be.

"Fine," he conceded. Andrew said it, but he knew it wasn't.

AFTER THE SHOW, Andrew slipped out of his seat and made for the stage exit. Throughout the show, he kept trying to make eye contact with Annabel, but she avoided looking at him whenever she faced his direction. He never meant to hurt her. He was doing this to protect her! Of course, she didn't know that

He weaved his way through the performers crowding the area and tried to spot the girl he wanted to talk to. He needed her to understand. It was too soon to lose her. He spotted her red hair as she wheeled herself out of the tent. Andrew made to follow but was met with the form of the ringmaster instead.

"Andrew—just the lad I was looking for." He placed a hand on the younger man's shoulder.

"Sir—" Andrew began, but he was cut off by another voice.

"Andrew! There you are." Valerie marched up to him. "You can't just run off without me," she huffed.

"And who is this?" William asked, features neutral as he watched the girl cross her arms.

Andrew opened his mouth to answer, but Valerie cut him off.

"What concern is it of yours?" she asked William. She turned to Andrew. "Why are you even talking to him?"

He clenched his jaw. "He's the father of the woman I love. The girl I'm trying really hard to see." He looked up at William. "Is Annabel in her tent? I've missed her greatly."

William frowned and scratched his chin. "May I speak to you privately, lad?"

Andrew nodded and followed William as he led him out of the tent. He had a bad feeling about where this was going.

"I must confess, I'm rather disappointed in you. I hate to see my little girl in tears, and that's what you brought her to today." The older man crossed his arms. The sleeves of his ringmaster's jacket tightened around his biceps, reminding Andrew that William was much stronger than he looked.

Andrew's heart lurched in his chest. He had made her cry? "I can explain that!" he blurted before taking a deep breath to calm himself down. "Please, sir. Let me explain."

William nodded. "If I'm not satisfied with your response, I will not let you see her. Do you understand?"

Andrew agreed. He could understand the man's position and had no issues with the terms. "It's to keep my parents from interfering. It was Valerie's idea, actually. They learned about what happened the last time I was here, and they were mad." He ran his hands through his hair and tugged on the strands. "Valerie intercepted me at the station when I arrived back in the city. She said my parents were furious with me, and she was hurt because I don't care for her like I do you. I really don't know where she got that idea from though." Andrew sighed. "She suggested we fake the relationship so my parents will take a step back, and that'll leave me free to come see Annabel." He added, "It will also keep Annabel safe. I don't know what lengths my parents would go to when it comes to their reputation. I don't want anything to happen to Annabel."

William rubbed between his eyes. "Well, at least I know you weren't setting out to hurt her. When I saw her crying, I was rather upset, you understand."

The young man hung his head. "I hate that I made her cry. I never intended to hurt her..." He floundered, unsure how to continue.

"I understand." The troupe leader rested a hand on Andrew's shoulder. "I think you're going about this the wrong way, and I think it will cause hardships. The Lord does not condone this kind of thing, but you have to work that out with Him yourself. So, I would just recommend proceeding with caution."

Andrew gave a half-smile and a nod.

"I will let you see her now. She's in her tent. I'm going to talk to this young lady you brought with you."

With that, Andrew took off as quickly as he could for Annabel's tent.

ELEVEN

Annabel hiked herself onto the bed in the corner of the tent. It had taken her quite some time to learn how to do that without help. The more she had started to train for her role in the troupe, the easier it had become to haul herself out of the chair and onto her bed using her arm and leg strength. She sprawled on the thick quilt and buried her face in the soft pillow. Tears pooled in the fabric below her. All she wanted was her happily-ever-after. Was that too much to ask for someone like her? Did God think she didn't deserve it? Annabel shook that thought away. That's not how things worked. Her father had always taught her that the Lord had a plan for her. He knew what was best for her, and whatever happened was for her good and His glory. She just needed to trust in Him and that plan.

Sometimes that was easier said than done though. And this was one of those instances. The sound of the tent flap moving caught her attention. She wiped her eyes before pushing herself up with her hands. She flipped herself over so she could see who was coming in. She expected her father or maybe even Amalia. What she wasn't prepared for was the sight of Andrew at the front of her tent. What was he doing here? "What do you want?" The question came out much harsher than she meant it to.

Andrew flinched but still made his way over to her. "Annabel…" His voice was broken and low.

"What? Haven't you had your fun? Make me fall for you only to stomp on my heart?" she asked.

Andrew shook his head. "No, not at all." He sighed. "I know you have no reason to listen to me, let alone believe me, but may I please explain what's happening to you? It's not as it seems." He reached out and tucked a strand of hair behind her ear. "I promise."

Annabel faltered. Did she want to hear his excuses? Would it make her feel any better? She couldn't see how it would, but the look on Andrew's face made her choose to listen. "Fine."

Andrew leaned forward, resting his elbows on his thighs. "Valerie, the girl you saw, is the woman my parents want me to marry. They've been pushing us together for some time now. After my last visit, they found out about you." Andrew buried his face in his hands before brushing his hair back. "I was worried about what they'd do to you. I don't know the lengths they're willing to go to keep the spotless image they have in society." He took her hands in his.

His hands were clammy in her grasp. She began to understand how difficult this was for him to talk about. How nervous he was about everything.

"When I got to the station on the mainland, Valerie was waiting there for me. She'd heard everything they said. At first she was angry because she thought I was in love with her." Andrew rolled his eyes. "I don't know how she came to that conclusion. After talking with her, she agreed to help me. So, to keep my parents off our trail, she and I are faking the relationship. She suggested this so I could see you."

He moved toward her and pressed his lips to her forehead before resting his own against hers. "I missed you so much."

Annabel gave him a soft smile. Everything made much

more sense now. But something still didn't sit right with her. What were Valerie's intentions? Did she genuinely want to help Andrew, or was she using this as a means to something else? So many concerns floated through her mind.

Annabel decided she could worry about that later. Truthfully, she had missed him too, and she could detect no insincerity from him. This was the course of action he thought would allow them to be together.

Annabel took Andrew's face in her hands. "I missed you too. I know we need to talk about this more, but for now, just know that I believe you. I don't approve of your plan, but I understand it at least."

He nodded, resting his hands on hers. "I'm so sorry for hurting you. I never wanted to do that." His grip on her hands tightened.

"Hush, it's all right now."

The tent flap opened, and three people walked through the entrance.

"I assume this means you have talked things over, yes?" William asked with a smirk.

Annabel and Andrew smiled at each other before turning to look at the group.

"Yes, Papa."

Andrew helped her into her chair and wheeled her over to everyone.

"I'm glad things are all worked out." Amalia ran her fingers through Annabel's hair.

Annabel didn't miss the frown on Valerie's face as she turned to face the rich girl.

"Hello," she held her hand out. "It's nice to meet you, Valerie. Thank you for helping Andrew and me."

Valerie stared at the outstretched hand for a minute before gingerly taking it and giving it a quick shake. Her brows were slightly furrowed, and Annabel could see a bit of scrunching in the bridge of her nose. She tried to hide it from everyone, but Annabel and her family made their living by reading people in different ways. There was no fooling them.

Andrew narrowed his eyes at the exchange, a little perturbed at Valerie's behavior. Was being polite that hard for her? He smiled to himself as he watched Annabel grin at Valerie. The high society girl was no match for the sweet girl. No one was immune to her kindness and open nature. This plan just might work. All he could do now was wait and see what the future held.

TWELVE

Some time had passed since Andrew and Valerie's first visit. He hoped he would have more time to spend with Annabel now that he and Valerie had this plan in place. He was quite disappointed to find that this was not the case. Valerie had them going everywhere: parties, the cinema, out for dinner. His life was dictated by social events and society affairs. Part of him couldn't help but wonder if maybe she was doing this on purpose, deliberately keeping him from the woman he loved. He was so tired of pretending for people whose entire lives felt like one enormous pretense. Everything was all about appearance and people's opinions. Why should his life be dictated by people who were so superficial? There would always be people who would be unhappy with him and his choices. Even spending time with his friends no longer held the same enjoyment it used to.

William had gifted him a Bible not too long ago, and he made sure to read it every evening before he went to bed. His eyes had been opened, and with each evening he read, he wanted to know more. He'd taken to writing questions down to ask the group when he got to visit again. Prayer became a regular part of his life.

Where do you want me to go, Lord? What do you want me to do?
Those questions haunted Andrew every waking moment. Was
Annabel his future? That seemed to be where the Lord was
guiding him, but how did one know for sure? It was a waiting
game for Andrew right now.

With a level of stealth any good thief would be proud of,
Andrew slipped out of the house and took off for Coney
Island. He was grateful for every little bit of time he got to
spend with her. This time, it would be without Valerie and her
never ending comments and social activities. He and Annabel
roamed the various parts of the island that was her temporary
home, starting with the vendors that lined the main walkway.
The weather was comfortable so they went from stall to stall
looking at all the wares the vendors had to offer. On more
than one occasion, Annabel had to stop him from buying
whatever her eyes lingered on for too long.

"Really, Andrew," she giggled, "you don't have to buy me
everything I stop to look at. I'm content to just look." She held
her hand over her shoulder, and he took it in his. "I'm just
happy to spend time with you."

Red tinted his face. The lady who ran the stall gave a small
laugh too.

"You two are just the sweetest. You remind me of my son
and his wife." Her eyes drooped a bit. "I lost them a few years
back to the influenza."

Annabel reached out and grasped the woman's hand. "I'm
so sorry."

Shaking her head, the woman held out the necklace that
had caught Annabel's attention. "Please take this. Young love
like yours is hard to find. I wish you both the best and all the
happiness in the world."

Annabel tried to insist she pay for it, but the lady wouldn't
hear of it. Andrew thanked her before clasping the chain
around Annabel's neck.

"It looks perfect." A small smile spread across his face.

They thanked the woman again before moving on. The memory replayed itself the entire way home for Andrew. He hoped they would have much happiness, but he also knew difficult times lay ahead. The charade would only last for so long.

He didn't know time was already running short.

———————

ANDREW RAN a hand down his face as he walked through the large wooden front doors of his home. The goal was to head upstairs and retire for the day, but luck was not on his side. As soon as he entered the foyer, Roger was there waiting for him.

"Your parents are waiting for you in the dining room."

Andrew groaned. "Can you tell them I've retired for the evening?"

Roger shook his head. "I'm afraid you can't get out of this one."

Frustration simmered within Andrew. What did they want now?

He mustered up every ounce of self-control he had to keep from stomping into the room like a petulant child. *I'd do it, too —if I thought it would work. Maybe they'd decide I'm too immature to marry Valerie.*

"Mother, Father. You wanted to see me?"

They sat on one side of their smaller table, meant for just the three of them at breakfast. Not that they ate together very often. His parents looked at each other before their gazes settled back on him.

"Yes. Have a seat, Andrew." His father gestured to the seat across from them.

His mother learned forward. "We've received some troubling news about you."

Dread pooled in the depths of Andrew's stomach. He

really hoped his suspicions about the news were wrong. He slid into the seat in front of him, his muscles rigid.

"What's this news you've received?" Andrew prayed his tone conveyed nonchalance, but he doubted he achieved it.

His father spoke first. "We've heard you've still been going to that nasty freak show on Coney Island."

"Not only that," his mother cut in, "but you've also been seen spending time with that disgraceful girl in the wheelchair."

Andrew took a deep breath. "Don't talk about her like that," he said through gritted teeth.

His mother scoffed. "How else should I describe her? She's a deformed freak preying on your naiveté and money."

Andrew shook his head. "She hasn't asked me for a single cent. She's not money-hungry like you are." His fists were shaking at his sides; his knuckles white from how tightly he clenched them. "Not everyone is obsessed with money."

Slamming his hand down on the table, Andrew's father stood up. "You will not speak to your mother and me like that. Do you understand me? If you continue to behave like this, I will disown you."

It was Andrew's turn to scoff. "Go right ahead. I don't care anymore. I'm done with this selfish and shallow lifestyle. I want no more of it."

He turned around and fled the room before his parents even had a chance to respond.

ANNABEL SAT at the mirror and brushed her hair, loosening the tangles left behind from twisting in the water. She hummed and smiled as she thought back on Andrew's visit the day before. He was kept away from her so she missed him greatly.

Annabel always tried her hardest to think the best of people, but when it came to Valerie, she really struggled. Why was she taking up so much of Andrew's time? This plan was supposed to allow Andrew and Annabel to have a little more freedom in spending time together. How long were they to wait in order to be together? She rubbed her eye and took in a shaky breath. She needed to trust God in this. He knew what was best for her, and she could always trust Him when it came to that.

"Annabel?" a voice called from the front of her tent. She turned around and saw her father standing there. His brows were furrowed, and he'd been biting his lip recently, judging by the cracks on his skin.

Annabel wheeled herself over to him and took his hand in hers. "Are you all right, Father?"

He nodded his head and gave her hand a squeeze. He ran his hand through his hair. "There's someone outside who wants to talk to you. He's going to ask you an important question, and I..." He took a deep breath, "I don't want you to feel like you have to say yes."

She tilted her head. "I don't understand."

"I love you, Annabel. You are my world and all I have left of your mother. Nothing could ever change that." He kneeled down beside her chair and pressed a kiss to her forehead.

She smiled and patted the top of his head. "I know, but I'm still confused about what's going on. Why did you need to tell me this, and why do you look so worried?"

He sighed, then stood up. "I'll send him in and let him explain."

Why was he so reluctant to tell her himself? What was so bad about what the man had to say that her father couldn't tell her himself?

A short, pudgy man walked through the flap of the tent, a top hat in his hand. He looked around and scrunched his nose.

She pushed down the urge to make a snide comment. That wouldn't be the right thing to do. She'd been raised better than that. Instead, she wheeled herself forward and greeted the man.

"Hello. My father said you wished to speak to me. How can I help you?" She held her hand out for him to shake.

He looked at her hand for a moment before shaking it. "Yes, hello, Miss…?"

"Annabel."

"Yes, Miss Annabel." He gave a slight nod. "I come with a business proposition for you." The man dabbed at his forehead with the handkerchief he pulled from his pocket.

She frowned. "Business proposition? For me?"

The man nodded, and his fingers drummed against the brim of his hat. "Yes. I've been sent on behalf of my client to offer you an opportunity to change your life."

She raised an eyebrow. "Change my life?"

"Yes. Yes. They're offering you the chance to have surgery to fix your legs. You'll be a normal person. Just like everyone else," he finished, wiping his brow again.

Annabel bit her lip. Was this really a possibility? She had no inkling this was truly an option for her. Surgeries had always sounded scary when she heard others talking about them. Maybe she was wrong. She was being offered the opportunity of a lifetime. She would be able to walk like a normal person. She could stroll by the sea with Andrew on one of their dates. This was an offer she really couldn't pass up.

But her father's face came to mind. He had looked so sad when he came in to announce the visitor. Did he want her to stay like this? Would he still love her if she weren't a mermaid? The questions weighed heavy on her heart.

"I can give you some time to think about it, if that would make your decision easier," the man offered.

Annabel nodded, thankful that she didn't have to decide right at that moment.

The man tipped his hat to her. "I'll expect your answer by the end of the week."

He pulled the flap aside and made his way out of the tent.

Annabel sat and stared at the spot he'd just been standing in. This was an opportunity to be with Andrew outside of their time here on the island. They wouldn't have to hide anymore. But could she do that to her family, to the people who had been there for her when no one else had. Was she willing to leave the show behind?

She fiddled with the hem of her shawl. Was this what she truly wanted?

The tent flap opened again, and Amalia strode in with a smile on her face.

"Penny for your thoughts?" she asked.

Annabel laughed. "I don't think they're worth that much."

Amalia shook her head, but her smile remained. "Your father told me about the offer. What are you thinking about it?"

Annabel sighed.

"I'm so torn. This is my chance to be with Andrew in a normal relationship." Annabel worried her lower lip. "I really love him, Amalia. I want this so much."

Amalia took Annabel's hand in her own. "I know, my dear."

"But I also really love my family. I have spent my whole life with this troupe. I don't want to leave you behind either." Annabel sniffled. "I don't want to have to choose."

Amalia squeezed Annabel's hand. "Who says you have to? We're your family. That will never change."

The corner of Annabel's mouth lifted. "You all will still love me?"

"There's nothing you could do that would make us stop loving you. The Lord has a plan for you, and maybe this is the next part of it." Amalia took Annabel's face in her hands. "No matter what the Lord has in store for you, we love you and are here to support you every step of the way."

"It's true!" a voice chimed in from the entrance.

The women turned to see her father standing there, but more faces were peeking in from the flaps.

Annabel smiled at them. "I could always strap my legs together. Then I could still perform." She scratched her cheek. "At least, I think I could. It wouldn't be as fluid. And I would have to learn to do it without drowning. I think it would feel different. Oh, but what if it doesn't work? I—"

"We love you, my little one. Whether you stay my little mermaid or not." Her father pulled her close to him and pressed a kiss to her head.

Tears sprang to her eyes. She hugged him back before wheeling herself to face the rest of her family to embrace as many of them as she could.

She had prayed her whole life for the chance to have normal legs. She'd never thought it possible until now. This had to be God's answer to her prayers over all these years.

Her mind was made up. She knew her path forward; all she had to do now was let the man know her decision.

THIRTEEN

Annabel smiled as she fixed her hair and smoothed her dress out. She'd been planning her look ever since Andrew wrote that he was coming to spend the day with her and take her on a date. She looked forward to seeing him and just passing the time together. Today was the day she'd tell him about the surprise. Nervousness had been her constant companion since he'd asked her to meet. His reaction could be good or bad, and that made her insides churn. She clipped on the bracelet he'd bought her before deciding she was ready.

Annabel wheeled herself out of the tent as Andrew strode up to greet her. He took her hand in his and kissed the back of it.

"You look beautiful."

Annabel's cheeks turned red at the compliment. "Thank you."

They made their way down to the waterline. Andrew took great care as he pushed her along the shoreline.

They stopped and admired the view every so often as the sun glistened on the water.

Annabel pulled her shawl tighter around herself, trying to battle the cold that felt icy against her skin.

Andrew noticed her shiver and wrap her arms tighter around her figure. He quickly shrugged off his suit coat and wrapped it around her shoulders.

"Is that better?"

Annabel turned her head to face him. "It is, but now you'll get cold!" She started tugging the jacket off, but he reached out a hand and stopped her.

"I'm fine. Besides, I'd rather be cold than see you uncomfortable."

His concern for her made both her heart and face warm. "Thank you." She pulled the coat closer and smiled when she smelled Andrew's unique pine scent radiate from it.

He bent down and pressed a kiss to the top of her head. "Anything for you. You have me wrapped around your finger."

She giggled and shook her head. She was thankful for moments with him like this. She could be herself and not worry about what anyone thought of her. Her family gave her the freedom to be herself, but she liked having someone outside the troupe that she could do this with.

They reached a perfect spot that offered a nice view of the ocean and protected them slightly from the wind. Andrew laid out the blanket he'd borrowed from William and spread it out on the ground. Annabel's eyes lit up when she saw him finish.

He turned to face her. "My lady." He held his hand out for her.

She smiled and placed her hand in his. He gently pulled her from her chair, allowing her to lean on him for support. He helped her down and seated her on the blanket. He plopped next to her and took her hand in his. She leaned into his side and rested her head against his shoulder.

"I'm glad we're able to spend time like this. I always miss it when you're away for a while." Annabel tilted her head up so she could see Andrew's face.

He gave her a smile and pressed a kiss to her forehead. "I miss it too. I wish I was able to make it out here more often." He threaded his fingers through her hair. "It's hard enough finding time to do anything at home anymore. Between my parents and Valerie, I barely have time to get enough sleep." Andrew snorted. "Though, I try to nap when Valerie makes me take her to the cinema. I don't think I've ever been so bored in my life."

Annabel shook her head. Andrew noticed the smile on her face didn't quite reach her eyes.

"What's the matter, my love?" he questioned. Worry gnawed on his insides; he hated seeing her unhappy, especially if he was the cause of it. "Have I said something wrong?"

Annabel shook her head. "No, you didn't say anything wrong. It's just..." she sighed and looked away. "It's nothing."

Andrew cupped the side of her face and moved her gaze back to him. "Please tell me what's troubling you. I can see if I can make it better."

The corner of her mouth twitched up. "You are the sweetest man I know." She kissed his cheek. "I've always wanted to go to the cinema, but I've never been able to go. My dad talks about when he'd take my mom there before the Great War." She leaned back against Andrew. "It's always been a dream of mine to go after hearing him talk about it."

"I'll just have to take you to one then." He took one of her hands in his and kissed the back of it.

Annabel shook her head. "It isn't a possibility right now."

Andrew's brows pulled together. "Why not?" he asked.

She fiddled with his fingers as she contemplated how to answer. "They don't like 'people of my sort in their establishments,' as the one man put it when my father last tried taking me."

Anger burned through Andrew at her words. How dare they deny her entry just because she was born with conjoined legs. It didn't make her any less human.

It felt like someone had dumped a bucket of cold water on him. Who was he to cast judgment? It wasn't that long ago that he thought that way about people like his Annabel. Guilt gnawed at his conscience. He was thankful for the change God had grown within him through his time with Annabel and the battles with his parents.

He looked down at the girl tucked into his side. Happiness engulfed him when he was with her like this. It was short lived. A frown tugged at his lips when he saw her playing with her fingers, something she only did when she was nervous.

He took her hands in his own. "Annabel, is everything all right?"

She looked up at him. "It's nothing. I thought I had something to tell you, but I've changed my mind."

Andrew's brows pulled together. "Annabel? You can tell me anything." He tucked a strand of hair behind her ear. "I won't judge you. I'm here for you."

She gave a small smile. "I know. Thank you for today. I've had a wonderful time."

Andrew wasn't entirely convinced, but he knew better than to try and push her. "I enjoyed being with you too. Any time with you is always enjoyable for me."

He helped her back into her chair, and they set off for her tent. Andrew felt like he should say something, but he had no idea what he should say. As they approached her tent, Andrew came to a halt.

"You know I love you, right?"

Annabel nodded. "Of course, I do. You've proven yourself many times over. I do not doubt your love for me."

Andrew knelt down before her and took her face in his hands. "Are you sure everything is all right?"

"Completely sure. I don't know what came over me earlier." She placed her hands over his. "I'm already looking forward to your next visit."

She felt like such a coward. She just couldn't bring herself to tell him, to possibly see the look of disappointment or disgust on his face. She knew her thoughts were irrational, but she couldn't help it. She'd spent so much of her life being mistreated and shunned by society that her fears had become too strong for her to overcome.

She pressed a kiss his cheek and bid him good night. Before she could enter her tent, Andrew called out to her. She turned to face him and was surprised to see that he was standing so close.

"I love you."

A genuine smile spread across her face, and she motioned for him to lean down. "I love you too." This time, she kissed his lips before wheeling herself into her tent.

Her sleep that night was fitful, but when she woke, she was firm in her decision.

It was time.

WHEN ANDREW AWOKE the next morning, a heaviness consumed his thoughts. Why was Annabel so nervous last night? What was she so afraid to tell him? Had he done something wrong?

So many questions swirled in his head. They gnawed at him as he headed downstairs for breakfast. He bit back a groan when he spotted Valerie at the table with his parents.

"Son, it's nice to see you this morning. Why don't you have a seat next to Valerie?" his mother prompted.

Andrew grumbled to himself but did as he was told. She gave him what Andrew guessed was supposed to be a charming smile. This was not how he wanted to spend his morning. The dread had not left him. He knew something bad was going to happen, but he didn't know what.

He played with his food at his breakfast. His mind was far away from whatever was taking place at the table. The image of Annabel from the day before was burned into his memory. He wanted nothing more than to be able to soothe her worries, but he didn't know what she had been fretting about. He frowned. Maybe he should sneak off and see her again today. He could try to wriggle the information out of her.

A hand on his shoulder ripped him from his thoughts.

"Andrew, is everything all right?"

Lost in his reverie, Andrew didn't know who had spoken, much less what the question had been. "I'm sorry?"

Valerie cupped his face and ran her thumb along his cheek. "Darling, are you feeling unwell?"

Andrew blinked at her. He was quiet for a few seconds before he realized he was supposed to answer her. "Oh, um. Actually, I am feeling a little under the weather. I think some fresh air might do me some good." He placed his napkin back on the table before standing and bidding those at the table farewell.

He decided today was a good day to take a drive. While of late he'd lost interest in most of what had occupied his time before he met Annabel, a drive sounded like just what he needed. It was a true testament to just how much his life had changed since he started spending his time with her family. He pressed the button and his car revved to life. He pulled onto the main road and headed toward the main part of the city. He pulled over when his friends on the sidewalk called out to him.

"Hey Andrew!"

He waved back to them, not wanting to seem rude. "Hey! How are you?"

He got a chorus of answers back. Everything from "Great!" to "All right, I guess."

Charles stepped forward. "We're heading down to the juice joint. We found one that's been playing jazz music. Don't be a flat tire!"

The first thought that came to his mind was whether or

not Annabel would like jazz music. If he knew where this club was, maybe he could take her there one night. Surely, they would be more accepting of her than most others. He thought it might be a nice outing.

"Sure! Hop in and tell me where to go."

The drive was filled with talk of the new film in the cinema, the flappers the boys had been spending time with, and more nonsense that Andrew didn't much care for. This used to be him, and now, he had better things to fill his time and his mind with.

The jazz music from the club was an interesting experience. It wasn't anything he had really put effort in listening to, but he was curious about what Annabel's thoughts would be. She loved new things. Her eyes would light up and whatever she was looking at would have her full attention.

How was she today? He hoped she was better than yesterday—that whatever was troubling her had passed.

When the boys got too rowdy, Andrew decided it was time for him to leave. He didn't need to get caught up in this kind of behavior. It would only lead to him getting into trouble.

He definitely did not need any more of that right now.

He strolled down the familiar streets. He wished Annabel could see how beautiful all the trees were here.

He slipped into the house and into his room without anyone noticing. He'd rather not deal with questions from anyone. He just wanted to stay in his room for the rest of the day. Maybe tomorrow would be a better day than today.

FOURTEEN

Andrew rolled over the next morning and groaned. Getting out of bed that morning did not sound like a good plan. Maybe he should just sleep a little longer.

The sound of the doorbell ringing defeated any chance there was of him falling back to sleep. He dressed quickly and rushed down the stairs. It was unusual for guests to arrive this early. Was it even early? He had absolutely no clue what time it was.

When he reached the hall, he spotted Roger standing at the door arguing with someone outside.

"Roger, is there a problem?" Andrew inquired.

Roger turned to face Andrew, a scowl on his face. "Sorry, Mister Andrew. There's someone claiming he must speak with you. He says he knows you, but I think it's a bunch of horse feathers."

Andrew raised an eyebrow. "What's his name?"

Roger opened his mouth, then closed it. He turned back to the man at the door and asked, "What did you say your name was again?"

Andrew heard a man groan on the other side of the door.

Something about his voice sounded familiar, but Andrew couldn't place it.

"It's William. Andrew, it's important."

Andrew's eyes widened. William? What was he doing here? What was important? He thought back to yesterday. Was it about Annabel?

"It's fine, Roger. I can handle this."

Roger spluttered. "But Mister Andrew—"

Andrew waved him off, and Roger, rather reluctantly, left Andrew to take care of the guest at the door.

Andrew led William out onto the porch on the side of the house and invited him to sit down on his mother's settee.

"What's going on, William? It must be serious if you came all the way to my home."

The older man ran a hand down his face and sighed.

This was the first moment Andrew had to really take in William's appearance. His normal clothes looked rumpled, and his eyes were bloodshot. The skin around his eyes was also splotchy, and his hair looked like Andrew's did after running his hands through it repeatedly. Andrew realized that's probably what had happened.

"Is something wrong?"

"I'm sorry to have just shown up like this, lad. I am fairly sure I must look rather scruffy right now. I apologize." William's voice was hoarse and rough.

"No need to apologize, sir. Do you need anything? I would invite you to come in," Andrew gestured towards the door, "but the staff is nosy. And they aren't afraid to report things to my parents."

William shook his head. "I've come here to give you some...some rather tough news." Tears began to spill down his face.

It was alarming for Andrew to see such a strong man cry right in front of him. "What is it, sir?" Andrew pressed.

William wiped his eyes with a shaky hand. "It's Annabel. She's dead."

Andrew stared at the man sitting across from him. "I'm sorry. What did you say?"

William rubbed at his eyes again. "My little girl is gone. We got the news this morning."

Andrew slipped out of his chair and his knees slammed into the porch.

Gone? How could she be gone? He'd just seen her the other day! She had seemed off that evening, but other than that, she was fine. How could she just be gone?

Andrew gripped his chest. The pain burning there made it hard to breathe. This couldn't be happening. His love was dead. His darling. His little mermaid. Dead. Gone. She was never coming back.

Andrew couldn't stop the cry that tore from his throat. His vision blurred, and he could feel the coolness of the air against the wetness trailing down his face.

He still had so much he wanted to do with her, so much he wanted to take her to see. All of that had been ripped away from him.

Arms wrapped around him and held him tightly. The feeling of someone else being there grounded him, and he allowed his body to succumb to everything he was feeling. His body heaved from the force of the sobs that pushed past his lips. He could feel William's hands patting his back. He appreciated the effort, but it brought little comfort.

Andrew didn't know how much time had passed, but his body finally just sagged, all energy spent. He was spent, through and through. He just wanted to crawl back into his bed and never wake up again.

William helped Andrew back up into his chair. Andrew

couldn't feel anything anymore. Sadness, grief, he couldn't feel any of it. Numbness had settled within his chest for an extended vacation, but Andrew doubted it was a temporary sensation.

Andrew inhaled, but it was weak at best. "What happened?"

William hesitated. "Did she tell you about the offer she received?"

Andrew shook his head. "Offer? What offer?"

William scooted forward to the end of his chair and leaned closer to Andrew. "We had a visitor the other day." He lowered his voice before continuing, "He seemed the type that works for families like yours."

Andrew sat back. "Families like mine? What do you mean?"

"Don't be offended. I didn't mean anything rude by it." William rolled his eyes. "What I was referring to was the way he dressed. You know, nice suit, fancy shoes. All of that."

Andrew nodded. "You mean like a lawyer."

"Exactly. He came to Annabel with an offer from a mysterious benefactor. He said they were offering her the chance to change her life."

"Change her life?" Andrew asked.

William ran his hand through his hair. Gray hid amongst the brunette hairs. He'd been right about William and the hair —as if it mattered. What did all this have to do with Annabel's death?

The older man sighed. "They offered her the chance to have an operation to fix her legs. To make her like everyone else. She boarded the last subway the night before last. The operation was somewhere here in the city."

Andrew sat all the way back in his seat. What? Who would offer her such a thing? The chances of the surgery ending successfully were so slim, it wasn't even worth it in the end.

Andrew rubbed the back of his neck. She shouldn't have taken him up on that offer. What was she hoping to gain?

Tears started streaming down his face again. He could feel the sting of the dry skin from his previous tears as the salty water came into contact with it. Was his love not enough for her? Had he not told her often enough how beautiful he found her?

Andrew ran his hand through his hair and tugged on the strands. Why hadn't she believed him? Had he somehow made her think otherwise?

Andrew had no words. He opened his mouth, but he couldn't even speak. He must be partially to blame for her choosing this. Should he have told her he loved her more? Could he have prevented this? So many questions threatened to drown him as he tried to unravel exactly what had happened. William's hand on his shoulder pulled him from the pit of his self-loathing.

"I can see what you're thinking. It wasn't your fault. She decided to accept the offer. Please do not blame yourself." William gave him a gentle smile. "I don't blame you."

Andrew sniffed in response. "Why would she do this? That's what I don't understand."

William bit his lip. "She's always wanted to be a normal girl. Even when she was little, she'd watch the children run by and want to join them." He fiddled with the hem of his coat. "Obviously, she never could, but she still tried. I used to get after her for wandering into that part of the town."

Andrew rubbed at his nose. "When's the funeral? Where are you burying her?"

"We're having a small service on the island next week. They never gave us her body, so I can't bury her," William choked out. "I can't even bury my little girl." His breaths grew short as his body heaved with his sobs.

This time, Andrew hugged him and let him cry. He didn't care who saw them.

William's cries grew soft, and he started to breathe normally again. They just sat there in silence for a few minutes, neither man knowing what to say.

So many questions, but few answers for them. The more Andrew thought about the whole situation, the more something didn't add up. People in high society didn't care about helping a poor girl with conjoined legs. Most of them only cared about themselves. So why would someone offer her this opportunity?

None of it made sense. The ice of his grief melted with the fire of his rage.

Who would play such a dangerous game with her life? Why wouldn't they let her father have her body to bury?

Andrew thought hard about who would have the most to gain in this situation. Who stood to benefit from her disappearance?

The answer came to him suddenly, and he rose from where he was seated. "I'm sorry, William, but I have to go. I need to know who did this."

William nodded, giving Andrew a pat on the back before turning to leave. He stopped at the door and looked at Andrew over his shoulder. "I hope you find them, son," he said.

"Me too."

William left, shoulders hunched.

Andrew turned on his heel and pushed his way inside.

"Roger!" he called out.

The man showed up about a minute later.

"You called, Mister Andrew?"

"Yes, Roger. Do you know when my parents should arrive home?" Andrew asked.

Roger stroked his chin carefully. "I do believe they said they'd be home this evening." Roger fixed his piercing gaze on Andrew. "Are you all right, Mister Andrew?"

Andrew ran a hand down his face. "Honestly, no," he

sighed. "My future has just been ripped away from me, and all my emotions are combining into one big mess."

He headed toward the stairs but stopped to look back at Roger. "Please tell my parents I wish to speak with them when they return."

Roger gave a nod, then Andrew went up to his room.

Pacing back and forth, he tugged at the strands of his hair.

Shock filled every thought swirling around in his head. She couldn't be dead. How could she be gone so suddenly? He'd just seen her a week ago.

It had been one of his favorite days they'd spent together. No worries, no interference, and nothing but the love they shared. It had been the first day for some time that Andrew felt truly carefree.

Andrew thought back on their final conversation. Her eyes had held something back. They had been bright when she had kissed him goodbye and said she couldn't wait for his next visit. But there had been that fidgeting nervousness that had consumed her for those few minutes.

She had said she had a surprise for him.

What surprise had she been talking about? Surely, this wasn't it.

Something was wrong about this whole situation. Why had it been her? Nothing made sense.

Thoughts rushed through his head, drowning him in grief and misery. The one question that kept popping up was: how could this have happened?

He had no answers and no clue where to start, but he needed to get to the bottom of this mystery. He needed to know what had led to her death, and why she was the victim. Everything suggested that what had happened was mostly likely planned out. Whether the intended outcome was her death, he didn't know. Nor did he know why they had chosen her of all people.

Did her kind heart make her an easy target? Was it

because of him? He would solve this and make sure the people responsible were brought to justice. It was the least he could do for her, and it was a way to distract himself from the pain of her loss and the void she left behind in his heart.

She hadn't deserved this fate. She had deserved the world and everything in it, but he couldn't give it to her now. Anger clashed and rolled with the grief inside him. A war of fire and ice with no clear winner.

He would solve this mystery.

He would find her killer.

Even if it was the last thing he ever did.

They wouldn't get away with it.

He threw himself on his bed and stared at the ceiling. He wanted to cry, but he couldn't produce any more tears. Instead, he focused on the numbness spreading through him. He couldn't feel a thing. Exhaustion overcame every part of him. He struggled to keep his eyes open.

Would his parents do this to her? The talk with his parents was all he could think about as he fell asleep.

FIFTEEN

Andrew woke up to someone knocking on his door. He groaned before rolling out of his bed. He tugged on his clothes, straightening them out.

"One moment," he called out.

He checked himself in the mirror, then went to the door.

Roger stood there, a blank stare on his face.

"Sorry, Roger." Andrew rubbed his eyes.

Roger merely sniffed in response. "Your parents have arrived home. I thought you'd like to know that."

Andrew nodded. "Thank you, Roger."

Andrew made his way down the stairs, stomach rolling at the thought of confronting his parents. He knew it needed to be done, but it didn't make the idea of it any easier. He heard voices coming from the dining room, so he decided to try there. Expecting his parents to be there, he was disappointed to find a couple servant girls cleaning and talking.

"Have you seen my parents?" Andrew asked.

The girls jumped at the sound of his voice and turned to face him.

One girl placed a hand on her chest. "You gave me a right scare there, Mister Andrew."

He apologized quickly. He really needed to find his parents. He spun around to look elsewhere, but the other girl called out, "They're on the porch."

He thanked the girls and took off to find his parents. His heart pounded as he skidded out the side door. There his parents sat, sipping tea and chatting as if nothing tragic had happened today.

They looked up at him as he made his noisy entrance.

"Are you feeling better, dear? Roger told us you weren't feeling well earlier." His mother only sounded mildly concerned.

Andrew shoved down the urge to roll his eyes. "I need to ask you a question. And I want an honest answer," he demanded.

They both looked quite shocked at his tone.

"What's so important that you feel the need to speak to us like that?" His father raised an eyebrow.

Andrew ran his hands through his hair. "Were you the ones who offered Annabel the dangerous surgery? Are you the ones responsible for her death?"

Part of Andrew wanted to sigh in relief at the look of genuine confusion on their faces. The other part of him was frustrated and confused because this was the only idea he could think of. Apparently, he had some detective work to do.

"What are you talking about, Andrew?" his father asked with furrowed brows.

Andrew wanted to scream in frustration. His father was telling the truth. Over the years, Andrew had learned how to tell when his parents were lying, and they weren't lying right now.

His mother set her teacup down and gave him her full attention. "Who is Annabel? What do you mean by dangerous surgery and her death?"

Andrew sat down in one of the chairs and buried his face in his hands. "I never stopped seeing the girl on Coney Island.

Valerie helped me come up with a plan to keep you guys from finding out we were still together." Andrew sniffed. "Her father came by this morning to tell me she was dead because someone had offered her a surgery to fix her conjoined legs."

"And you think we did such a preposterous thing?"

Andrew lifted his head up to look at them. "The person who came to give her the offer looked like someone's lawyer, and who else would be able to afford that kind of surgery?"

His parents shared a look.

"Why would we have done something to make your ridiculous infatuation with her easier?" his mother questioned.

"Anyway, this all works out for the best. You two wouldn't have lasted. Now you can move on with Valerie, without distractions."

His father's words ignited a fire within him. "Do you not care at all that the woman I love just died? Does my pain mean nothing to you?"

The man just blinked at him. "You wouldn't have lasted, son. Her kind need to stay in their place. They don't fit in with our society. Whoever offered her this surgery did you a huge favor."

Andrew wanted to say something, but it would get him nowhere. Arguing with them was pointless as they would never see things his way.

He spun on his heel and marched inside. He grabbed his hat and coat before stomping out the front door and out onto the street.

"Where are you going?" his mother called after him.

Andrew stopped and looked over his shoulder at her. "Away from here. I can't believe the two of you. I'd rather not sit in company with people who try to convince me the death of my love is for the better."

Without another glance, he went straight to the subway station. He heard someone calling his name along the way. He didn't know who it was, and he didn't care. This city cared about no one but themselves. They had no compassion, no love, and no heart. Why couldn't these people just open their eyes to the struggles of their fellow men? Why couldn't they see that while they obsessed over societal expectations and positions, others had to exploit their differences just to survive?

Andrew settled in his seat on the subway car. Leaning back, he arranged his hat so it covered part of his face and closed his eyes. How badly he wanted to run away—maybe join up with her troupe, her family. The coldness had returned, pumping through his veins faster than blood. He would never again get to hear her singing to herself when she thought he wasn't paying attention. He wouldn't get to watch her dance through the water. No more admiring her as she brushed out the tangles the water had left behind in her hair. It was all gone. All he had now were memories. His maudlin side insisted old age would eventually steal those from him too.

What he wouldn't give to have her be a part of his world once more.

ANDREW STEPPED off the subway car and onto the familiar Coney Island road. It used to bring him comfort and happiness, knowing he was so close to seeing her. All of him wished the conversation with William had been a dream—that when he got to her tent, he'd hear her singing away as she brushed her hair. The closer he drew to the tents, the more his heart filled with dread. The faces of the troupe members he passed told him all he needed to know.

It hadn't been a dream. She was really gone.

Swallowing grew more difficult as his vision blurred with tears. Now was not the time for crying. He needed to be strong. Annabel always put her family first, and now Andrew would do that for her. He would help and comfort them in any way he could. A tragedy of this magnitude was not something he'd ever experienced before. *Please Lord, help me to help them,* he prayed. He couldn't do it on his own, but with the Lord's help, he could. And he would.

He heard noises coming from inside Annabel's tent. Who was in there? He peered through the flap and spotted Amalia sitting on Annabel's bed with her face in her hands.

Not wanting to disturb her, Andrew crept as quietly as he could into the tent. He just stood there and let her cry. It was better for her to get it all out than for him to interrupt her. His legs started to go numb with the long wait, but he chose to push through the pain. This is what her family needed, and he would do his best to provide.

Amalia sniffled, wiping her eyes. Her head lifted up, and she let out a small scream, hand flying to her chest, eyes wide.

Andrew held his hands up, handkerchief in one hand. "Sorry, I didn't mean to frighten you. I wanted you to be able to finish having a good cry. To let it all out." He handed her the handkerchief.

She took it and nodded her head. "Thank you. That was very kind of you." She dabbed her eyes, then blew her nose. Stuffing it in her pocket, she said, "I'll wash this and give it back to you."

Andrew shook his head. "You keep it. Never know when it might come in handy."

William ran into the tent. "What's wrong?" He was panting and sweat poured down his face.

Amalia gave a hearty laugh when she looked him over. "Nothing's wrong. Andrew just frightened me is all. I didn't see him standing there."

Andrew smiled sheepishly at him.

William stood there, chest still heaving. "Andrew? What are you doing here?"

Amalia faced him too. "Yes, I'm assuming you came here for a reason?"

"I needed to get out of my house. I couldn't stand being around my parents right now."

She gestured at the spot next to her. "That's understandable. How are you holding up? I know this can't be easy for you either."

Andrew sat down next to her with a sigh. William sat down on the other side of Amalia.

"I don't think my mind has fully grasped that she's gone. I just keep cycling through the same questions," he answered.

Amalia nodded. "I keep doing the same thing. So many details don't make sense to me."

"For me as well. What question keeps haunting you the most?" William added.

Amalia faced him. "Why won't they let us have her body to bury?"

Andrew had already forgotten about that. It was rather odd. Why would they need to keep her body unless they had something to hide? Andrew rubbed at his jaw line. "That is strange. I have so many questions about who and why, but I have no answers for any of it."

Amalia reached over and patted his shoulder. William reached over to Andrew and did the same on his back.

"I thought maybe my parents had offered her the operation, but there was genuine confusion on their faces. I've learned to tell when they're lying, but they were telling the truth when they said they took no part in the operation scheme." He rubbed at the back of his neck. "That was the only idea I had, but it got me nowhere."

Amalia bit her lip. "Maybe it's time to look elsewhere. If the troupe pools our money together, we might have enough to pay for a private investigator to look into her death."

Andrew straightened up. "Why didn't I think of that? I'll pay for it, and I'll find someone in the city who can help us."

The others shook their heads. "We want to help too.

Please let us give some money for it too. It won't be much, but it's something."

Andrew wanted to say no, but he knew how important this was for them. They didn't have much money, and he had more than enough to afford it. The idea of taking even a little bit of their money just didn't feel right to him. How would he feel if it was reversed? Andrew didn't have to contemplate on it for long at all. If it was his daughter, he'd do anything he could. They needed this as much as he did. So he stamped down the desire to just do it himself and accepted the offer of help.

"I'll start looking for someone tomorrow. The sooner we get answers, the better. It'll leave the guilty party less time to get rid of anything that might incriminate him." Andrew pulled out his pocket watch and checked the time. "The last car has already left. I'm sorry for imposing, but would it be fine if I stayed here tonight?"

William stood up. "I have a spare cot in my tent. You can sleep there for the night. It's the least we can do for you." He laid a hand on Andrew's shoulder. "Thank you for loving my daughter and for being willing to help us find out what happened to her."

Andrew gave a half smile. "She always went out of her way to help others. Now, I want to do that in honor of her whenever and however I can. I will carry the torch in her stead. If you ever need anything, please don't hesitate to come to me. I will help however I can."

Amalia stepped forward and hugged Andrew tightly. She waved at William to join them. The hug they gave him filled him with warmth. Was this what it felt like when one had parents who showed affection? It was a sensation he knew he would have to get used to. Amalia let him go, gave him a warm smile, then left the tent.

William guided Andrew out and to the left. The two men

walked in silence until they reached the tent that William and Levi shared.

"It'll be a little cramped, but it'll do."

Andrew shook his head. "I just appreciate you letting me stay. I'm grateful for whatever you can give me."

The two men entered the sleeping quarters, and William dug around for something that Andrew could wear. "These should fit you."

After they were both ready for bed, William pointed to the cot Andrew would be sleeping in. "That'll be your bed for the night. Sleep well, lad. If you need anything, just wake me up."

Andrew gave a nod. "Thank you, William. Good night." With that, the lights were extinguished.

Andrew fell asleep that night thinking about who he could go to for help. There had to be someone he could trust to get them the answers they needed.

SIXTEEN

Andrew got on the first subway the next morning. He made a quick stop by his house to clean up and pick up his car. It took every ounce of courage he possessed to ignore his parents' interrogations about where he had been the night before. Telling them he had spent the night with the troupe would only antagonize them further. Instead, he told them that he had been with friends.

That ordeal over, Andrew hopped in his car and drove to meet with his banker. Business there first, and then he'd go visit an unfamiliar part of town—one where he'd find an investigator.

The bank was an altogether unpleasant experience. When he'd asked to withdraw his money, the banker gaped.

"I'm sorry, sir. You wish to withdraw all your money?"

Andrew shoved down the urge to roll his eyes. "Yes."

This was a crucial step in his plan. He wanted to put as much distance between him and his parents as he could financially. They wouldn't be able to keep him from his money this way.

The man stood still, mouth opening and closing like a fish. "But sir…" he spluttered.

"I'm sorry, but I'm in a hurry." Andrew drummed his fingers on the counter.

The man looked at his manager, then back at Andrew. This, of course, caught the attention of the manager and brought him over.

"Is there a problem here?"

Andrew wanted to groan but kept it together so he could answer. "Well, yes. I want to withdraw my money, but this man seems to take offense to that."

The manager looked at Andrew, then at his employee. "Please excuse us for a moment, sir."

They stepped away and conversed for a moment. Andrew didn't have time for this. His parents wouldn't be happy if they knew he was doing this, and the longer this took, the more his stress built. His hands were sweaty, and his heart felt like it would burst from his chest.

When they came back, Andrew was ready to leave. It wasn't supposed to take this long just to get his money.

"Excuse me, sir, but are you sure you want to pull this money out?" the manager asked.

Andrew wanted to strangle him, but that wasn't the right thing to do here. After taking a deep breath, he answered. "Yes, and I'm in quite a hurry, if you don't mind."

"This is quite a large sum to be pulling out..." he trailed off.

Poor Andrew was sure there was a prominent vein on his forehead at this point. He needed to make sure he didn't forget what he had learned about showing Christ to others. It wouldn't do him any good to be rude right now. "Yes, and I have my reasons for pulling it out."

The man opened his mouth but decided whatever he had to say wasn't worth it. He nodded and started the transaction, glancing up at Andrew every so often.

Andrew tried not to draw attention to himself as he left the bank by walking at the same pace as everyone else who exited beside him. There was a smaller bank just down the street that would perfectly suit Andrew's needs. He took the money his parents had given him over the past few years and managed to get it all into an account that his parents couldn't touch. At least if they disowned him now, he'd have some money to live on. He knew a storm was brewing between him and them, so he needed to be prepared for the consequences.

Andrew maneuvered his way around the slight bit of traffic and into Manhattan. He parked far enough away to avoid any suspicion should anyone he knew be hanging around in this part of town. The walk did him good. He needed a chance to get his thoughts in order before trying to explain everything to the private investigator. Everything that had happened up to this point overloaded his thoughts, so much so that he forgot to pay attention to his surroundings.

"Oomph!" The wind was knocked out of him as he collided with something.

"Sorry about that!" a voice said.

Or someone apparently. Andrew stood up and brushed himself off. "No, no. It was my fault. I wasn't watching where I was going. I apologize." Andrew gave the man a smile that was returned.

As Andrew took a good look at the man, he realized he had to be an investigator. His outfit consisted of the recognizable hat and trench coat. He couldn't believe his luck!

"Excuse me, sir. Do you happen to be a private investigator?"

The man's smile slipped. "Why are you asking?"

"I need to hire someone to help me. It's urgent." Andrew took a few steps forward, desperation oozing out of each step. "Please."

The man raised an eyebrow. "Urgent? What, your girl cheating on you, and you want to find out who the man is?" He scoffed. "I really don't think that classifies as urgent."

Andrew shook his head. "No! I need to know how she

died. I need to know who sent her to her death." Andrew's voice went from loud to a hoarse whisper. He just wanted someone to help him. That's all he needed. "Please."

The man scrutinized him for a few moments. Andrew shifted his weight under the man's intimidating gaze.

"What's your name, kid?"

"Grayson. Andrew Grayson."

The man nodded. "I'm Mark Westley." He held his hand out.

Andrew took it and gave it a firm shake. "It's good to meet you."

The man gave another nod and motioned for Andrew to follow him. They walked about a block down before Mark stopped in front of a small building, pulled out a key, and unlocked the door. The door clicked open, and Mark led him inside.

Andrew looked around at the newspaper clippings on the wall. It looked like this man had solved his fair share of cases. The hope inside Andrew burned a little brighter.

"So, tell me about your case."

Andrew turned and found Mark behind his desk and pointing to the chair in front of him. He sat down and began his story. He went through every detail he could think of, including what William and Amalia had told him, doing his best to make sure nothing was left out. Andrew poured his heart into it, needing to know who did this. If the answer couldn't be found, it would not be because of him.

"What happened to the man that was following you?" Mark asked.

Andrew paused his story and stared at Mark. "I'm not quite sure. I haven't seen him following me since."

Mark nodded and wrote something down in his notebook. After a few moments of silence, Mark looked up. "Continue."

Andrew scratched his temple. "Oh, yes."

Of all the questions he stops to ask, that's the one he chose?

Andrew shook his head but continued on with his story. When he reached the end, Mark hummed.

"This is quite the case you've got here. There's a lot going on, for sure. I'll need to get some details from the others so I know who I'm looking for."

Andrew's eyes lit up. "Does this mean you'll take the case?"

The corner of Mark's mouth twitched up. "Yes, kid. You're a strange one, but I can see how much you loved your girl. I will do my best to find out what happened to her. You have my word."

Andrew shot out of his chair and shook the man's hand with such vigor that it rattled the man's glasses slightly askew.

The man chuckled. "Calm down, lad!"

"Sorry! I just, I can't tell you how grateful I am for this."

Mark waved him off. "I'll visit her family this week and get more information from them. I'll send you updates when I can."

"How much do I owe you for your time today?" Andrew pulled out his wallet.

Mark shook his head. "You can pay me if I find anything that's helpful in finding out what happened to her. If I can't find anything, my time is free."

"But—"

"No. What's happened here should be investigated by the police, but I know how they view the people on Coney Island. I will do my best to help you find the answers."

Andrew shook the man's hand. "God bless you, sir."

"You too."

The two men parted ways, and Andrew walked back to his car. Hopping in, he stopped on the way back to send a note to William, letting him know they were making progress and apprising him of the future visit from Mark.

When he returned home, he heard three distinct voices

coming from the drawing room. Andrew groaned. What was *she* doing here?

ANDREW WALKED into the drawing room and noticed his parents and Valerie chatting and sipping tea.

"Good afternoon," Andrew greeted as he stepped into the room.

The three looked up at him and stopped talking.

"Hello, Andrew." His mother stood up and crossed the room to him.

She held her arms out for him, and he hugged her, his body stiff. "Hello, Mother."

She pulled him over to sit with the others. His father wouldn't meet his gaze, and Valerie wrapped her arm around his with a sad expression.

"I'm so sorry to hear about Annabel." Her bottom lip jutted out, making her look like a new species of fish.

Andrew held back a snort.

"Um, thank you, Valerie." He pried his arm from her grasp and moved over a smidge. Andrew had no interest in continuing the charade with Valerie. She had to know that by now. Did she actually think Annabel's death would mean he was "over" her and would be interested in Valerie again?

Valerie moved over so she was closer again. "Aw, Andy, don't be like that."

Andrew pulled himself away from her and stood up. "I think I'll go for a walk. Good evening, Valerie, Mother, Father."

"Wait, son," his father called out.

Andrew stopped in the doorway, then looked over his shoulder at everyone. "Yes?"

His father motioned him over. It was difficult not to huff

and sag his shoulders, but he managed to resist. He turned back and dragged himself over to the group.

"Sit down." The man pointed a finger at the open spot next to Valerie.

This time, Andrew did huff, but he still sat down.

"You better watch your tone with me, boy."

Would rolling his eyes count as a tone? He decided he didn't want to find out. "Yes, Father."

Andrew watched as his father stroked his chin; his gaze felt sharp on the two of them. Valerie shifted in her seat. He just wanted to get this over with, but he knew better than to push the boundaries.

"We've already lost too much time on this wedding." His father stared at him. "I'm sorry your little friend died. There's nothing you can do about it now, so it's time we move forward with this wedding."

Andrew opened his mouth to protest, but he was instantly cut off.

"No. There will be no arguments. You will do as you are told."

Valerie wrapped her arm around his again. "Oh, come on, Andy. We'll get along just fine. You'll learn to love me eventually."

Andrew tugged on her arm, but she wouldn't budge. Why couldn't she take the hint that he wasn't interested? He continued to struggle to pry her off. Eventually he decided to give up trying and wait for her to loosen her grip.

Andrew's mother spoke, "It doesn't give us much time, but we want the wedding to be in two months. I've already started planning with your mother, Valerie."

She squealed. The sound made him want to cover his ears. He didn't know women were capable of making such a high-pitched sound. It wasn't something he ever wanted to hear again.

At the risk of getting snapped at by his father again, he chose not to rub his ear. It throbbed slightly.

The two women had delved into wedding plans and decoration ideas that he couldn't care less about. Andrew sat there staring down at the floor. Did he even matter to them anymore? He had just lost the woman he loved, and they'd already begun planning his wedding to someone else — someone he didn't even *like*. It all came to a boiling point when his father clapped a hand on his shoulder.

"We'll get this wedding on in no time. Then you'll finally be married and set for life. No more needing to pine over that freak show girl."

Andrew shot out of his seat. "Don't talk about her like that! You can't make me marry Valerie. I won't do it."

His mother leaned forward and placed her hand on his arm. "Honey, you can't stay a bachelor for the rest of your life."

He pulled away from her. "I can and I will. I won't forget Annabel just because she died and you want me to get married. I will spend the rest of my life loving her, and no one else."

With that, he stormed out of the room.

He couldn't believe his family could be so cold and callous. A girl had died—someone important to him, no less—and they acted as if it were inconsequential.

Andrew just kept walking. He had no specific destination in mind. He just wanted to get out of that house. He looked at those around him. Businessmen rushed past people. Families smiled and huddled together. Couples strolled arm in arm, adoration for the other clear in their eyes. That made his heart clench. What he wouldn't give to be able to push Annabel along in her wheelchair, the two of them talking and laughing like everyone else. Instead, he was left behind, alone. Her absence left a huge hole within him. One she had managed to create all too quickly.

After walking several blocks, Andrew's stomach growled. He craved a hot dog from Coney Island, and that thought brought longing for a place where he felt accepted. Would they let him stay again? He didn't want to presume too much on their hospitality, but he knew they wouldn't mind.

He would visit when he received the first piece of news from the investigator. Would the man find any answers to his questions? He couldn't bear wondering what had happened to her for the rest of his life. Andrew tried not to dwell on it, but he couldn't find much else to focus on. He needed answers, and he hoped he would get them. He just needed to have patience and trust God.

He could do that. Couldn't he?

SEVENTEEN

It was a week before he heard anything from Mark. The man sent a note in the mail saying he had a lead on who had performed the surgery. As soon as he got the letter, Andrew dashed for his car and made his way down to Mark's office. Andrew knocked on the office door, and a squat, blonde woman opened it.

"May I help you?" she asked him.

"Yes, I'm here to see Mr. Westley."

The woman raised an eyebrow. "I'm sorry. Mr. Westley is very busy. If you come in, you can leave the details of your case for him to review."

Andrew ran a hand through his hair. "I'm here because he's already taken my case. I received a note from him about it this morning."

"Ah, young Mister Andrew. Please come in. I have your information here," a voice from behind the woman said.

She moved out of the doorway and let Andrew pass. She huffed as she took her seat, clearly displeased with the whole exchange.

Mark led him into the room at the back. He sat down behind the desk and pointed to the chair in front of him.

"Please excuse Margaret. She runs a tight ship here." He laughed.

Andrew gave a small smile.

"Sit," Mark said.

Andrew did as he was told. "You said you had a lead on what happened to Annabel."

Mark filed through some papers on his desk, trying to find the one he was looking for.

"Yes, ah, here it is." He held up a paper and put his spectacles on before continuing. "I've found the surgeon who performed the operation on your Miss Annabel."

Andrew sat forward in his seat. "You did?"

"Yes," Mark answered and nodded.

That light of hope within Andrew burned brighter at this. His insides felt fluttery to the point of nauseousness. "What did he say?" His breathing pace sped up, and he gazed intently.

He was so close. He would finally get his answers. It was just a matter of how long he had to wait for them.

"The man's name is Harvey Griffith. Have you ever heard of him?"

Andrew thought back on conversations with his parents, friends, and anyone he had met while attending society functions with Valerie.

"Sorry, but the name doesn't sound familiar at all to me. Should it?" Andrew sincerely hoped the answer was no. If he somehow knew this man, he'd never forgive himself.

Mark shook his head. "I don't think so. I've investigated this man before. I'm not surprised he's involved here."

"Did he tell you who hired him?" Andrew inquired.

"I haven't talked to him yet. I just got this information yesterday morning. I'll try to catch him this afternoon."

Andrew nodded. "I won't delay you any longer. Thank you, truly, for all your hard work." He held out his hand.

"We'll figure out what happened. I feel very confident

about that." Mark placed his hand in Andrew's and gave it a firm shake.

Andrew attempted a smile. He ducked through the doorway and exited the building. A bit of the fog of grief rolled back, and he could think better. Now it was time to tell her family.

Andrew navigated his way back home, grateful for the lack of traffic on the road. His shoulders sagged when he walked into the house and found his parents and Valerie there. He couldn't remember a time his parents had been home so much at any other point in his life. He tried to drop off his car keys without being intercepted, but he wasn't that lucky.

"Andy!" Valerie squealed.

He rolled his eyes, unconcerned about being scolded as his back was to them.

"Hello, Valerie." His tone was terse, clearly communicating he didn't want to talk.

Either she didn't get it, or she chose to ignore it. Andrew didn't really care which one it was. He just wanted to get out of there. He needed to get to William and Amalia. He wanted to tell them the name of the surgeon who shared responsibility in Annabel's death.

He edged closer to the door, but his parents joined them before he had the chance to escape.

"Son, where are you off to at this time of day?" His father and mother stepped into the room with frowns on their faces.

Andrew groaned.

"Excuse me, young man. Don't you dare take that attitude with your mother," his father snapped.

How is it that the tone of his voice still sent a chill down Andrew's spine? They were expecting him to get married, yet he still quavered at his father's scolding. He knew better than to press right now. He needed to tread carefully.

"I have some business I need to take care of. I'm sorry, but I'm in a hurry." With that, Andrew headed for the door. He needed to know if William and Amalia knew this man or even knew of him. He couldn't waste time by waiting until tomorrow.

"Come back here!"

Andrew didn't listen. His goal had now become to get to William and Amalia. He opened the door and stepped out onto the porch. Glancing over his shoulder, he saw that his parents and Valerie followed behind him. He slammed the door shut and took off down the street, determined to get out of sight before they came out the door.

He ducked between two buildings on the street. Taking a few steps back, he hid in the shadow before they passed by. They were searching for him. Once they turned around and went back towards the house, Andrew bolted from his hiding spot and slipped around the corner.

He didn't remember taking a breath until he was finally on the subway car and on his way to the island. Panting, his heart rate calmed, and his stomach slowly unknotted.

Andrew thanked God as he stepped out into the cool, salty air, letting it fill his lungs and his heart. He loved seeing those red tents against the blue and pink backdrop of the ocean and sunset. It was a place he had once wished to make his home, but it wouldn't be the same without her. Would the troupe even want him if he asked to join them? What would he even do?

His feet led him down the path to the main tent. He could hear William's voice shouting from the inside.

"Thank you, ladies and gentlemen, for joining us for a magical evening! I bid you all farewell!"

The crowd gave a loud gasp. Andrew smirked. He knew that meant that William had pulled his disappearing act. He wanted to learn how to do that. It would help make his getaways quicker when he needed to sneak out of the house.

Andrew walked around to the back of the tent. There used to be loud chatter amongst the troupe after each show, but now only muted whispers marred the relative silence. The atmosphere was somber. He ached for the way her laughter would fill the air and bring prompt smiles to even the grumpiest of faces.

He turned the corner and waved at Levi resting against one of the larger prop boxes. Levi nodded in reply. Andrew didn't know him very well, but he enjoyed the conversations they had. Aside from her father and Amalia, Annabel had been the closest to Levi. Though not related by blood, they treated each other as siblings.

"How are you?" Andrew asked.

Levi gave a quick wipe of his eyes. "I'm just trying to get used to her being gone."

Andrew set a hand on his shoulder. "I understand. If you ever need to talk, I'm here."

Levi's mouth twitched. "Thank you. I'll keep that in mind."

A voice sounded from the back entrance of the tent. "Andrew, my boy, it's good to see you. What are you doing here?"

William, still clad in his staple red outfit, stepped out and joined the conversation.

"Willam," Andrew gave a quick nod, "it's good to see you too. I come bearing news."

William's eyes lit up, and he patted Andrew's back with a little more force than he thought was necessary.

"I have some questions for you too."

William had questions for him? Andrew didn't like the sound of that. Had he done something? He followed William into Annabel's tent. The sight of her belongings strewn about hinted that they might be in the process of cleaning it out.

"What news do you have?" William turned and asked Andrew once they were safely tucked away in the tent.

Andrew sat down in one of the chairs while William settled in a chair across from him. "The private investigator found the doctor. His name is Harvey Griffith. Does that name mean anything to you?" Andrew hoped William might have some lead on this man, but William shook his head.

"I can't say I've ever heard that name. What did he say to Mr. Westley?"

"He hasn't talked to him yet. He's looking to do that this week." Andrew scratched at the side of his face.

William sighed. "Well, we can only hope he'll find something."

Andrew nodded. "You said you had some questions for me?" He needed to know what was going on. His stomach hurt from the knots that had settled there.

"Ah, yes." William pulled out a pack of what appeared to be letters from the bag on the bed. "Did Annabel tell you anything about receiving any letters?"

Andrew pursed his lips and furrowed his brows. "I don't recall her ever mentioning that. Why do you ask?"

William handed him the pack in his hand. With great curiosity, Andrew took them and opened the one on top.

STAY AWAY FROM ANDREW. THIS IS YOUR FINAL WARNING.

Andrew's hands trembled as he gazed down at the note. He went through a few of the letters and found the same types of threatening messages. Tears stung at his eyes. How long had she been enduring this because of him? His insides twisted and rolled at the thought that she was being harassed because she was close to him. She didn't deserve this kind of treatment, especially not because of him. Most importantly though, why hadn't she said anything to him? Hadn't she trusted him?

"How long has she been receiving these?" Andrew asked, his voice raspy.

The older man shrugged. "I didn't even know she was getting letters. She never told anyone. I've asked Amalia and Levi. They both said she never told them either."

Andrew ran his hands through his hair and tugged on the strands. "Why would she keep this from us? Didn't she trust us?" The tears started to fall. "Didn't she know I would have helped her?"

Sobs racked his body, and his breathing grew ragged. He needed her back. He had so many questions for her, so many things he wanted to know. Why did she have to have that stupid surgery? Why couldn't she have just been happy as she was—with him? The selfishness of that thought stunned Andrew. It wasn't his life to live. Who was he to condemn her decision?

William crouched down and pulled Andrew close to him.

"It'll be okay, son. She had her reasons for this. The Lord has His reasons for this as well. All we can do is trust." He patted Andrew's back. "The Lord knows best. We can rest on that."

Andrew nodded into the older man's shoulder. "Sorry. That was selfish of me. I know you're grieving too."

William leaned back and gripped Andrew's shoulders. "Don't apologize, lad. We all need support when we go through trials like this. It's true I lost my daughter, but that doesn't mean you can't grieve the loss of your love."

Andrew took a deep breath.

"You know something else?" William asked. "Though I lost my daughter, the Lord has blessed me with a son." William gave him a smile. "Annabel would want us to move on together and honor her memory rather than sit and be sad like this."

The young man's lips twitched in a half smile, tears flowing once more. "Thank you, William. You all have never failed to make me feel loved and wanted."

William ruffled his hair. "God has given us a lot of love to share. When you have little, you have a lot to give."

Andrew wiped his nose and stood up. "Would you mind if

I took these to give to Mark? He might be able to connect the author of these to the surgery offer."

William nodded and walked with Andrew back to the station. "Peace be with you, son."

Andrew smiled, "You as well."

With that, he boarded the subway and set off for home, the letters heavy in his pocket.

EIGHTEEN

"**W**here have you been?" His mother's voice echoed in the entryway.

"I was visiting a friend."

Andrew closed the door and turned to face her.

She stood there with her arms crossed, and his father mirrored her stance. Valerie stood off to the side, watching the scene unfold. "You were out rather late for visiting a friend. And we know it wasn't that mermaid freak you were seeing, given that she's dead."

Fire burned in Andrew's core. How dare they speak about her like that! "Don't talk about her like that! She doesn't deserve that kind of treatment."

Valerie scoffed, "Andy, darling, she doesn't deserve anything. She's poor and deformed, which makes her doubly tragic, don't you think?"

His fists clenched at his side, while his body shook with the force of his anger.

"Setting that aside, the wedding date has been set. You will marry Valerie in a month's time, whether you like it or not." His father took a step forward. "This is what's best for you and for this family."

"No!" Andrew shouted.

Six eyes widened. Andrew had never spoken to his parents like that, but he was done. This was his life to live, and his love to choose.

"Excuse me?"

"You heard me, Father. I've let you dictate my life for far too long. You three are horrible people, and I don't want any part of it."

He looked at Valerie, "I'm sorry, Valerie, but I don't love you, and I don't think I could ever learn to. We are just too different."

Her lip trembled, "You can't do this to me! I've worked too hard to make you mine. This isn't what's supposed to happen!"

Andrew wanted to cover his ears at the pitch of her screech.

His mother rushed to Valerie's side. "Don't worry, my dear. We'll get this sorted. The wedding will still go on. We'll bring him around."

Andrew's father rubbed at his forehead. "Go to your room, you won't be leaving there until you've come to your senses. We'll have food sent to your room."

Andrew wasted no time in bounding up the stairs. He didn't want to be there a second longer.

He threw the door of his room open and slammed it shut behind him.

With a small leap, he plopped onto his bed, his nerves still buzzing from his encounter with his parents and Valerie. What kind of parents did this to their child—their *grown* child, no less? This wasn't a family he wanted to be a part of any longer.

ANDREW PACED along the length of his room. *There has to be more to this whole situation than what meets the eye.* He'd been like this for most of the morning and afternoon. Roger chastised him for only picking at his food that morning. Taking care of himself was not on his list of priorities that day. *Lord, I know you have a plan, but I'm not sure what to do. Please guide me.*

There had to be some clue he missed. Something someone said or did that would help him solve the mystery. His parents just wanted to push him into marriage with Valerie, but that was the only thing that he could hold against them in this situation. So, who else was there?

"It wasn't supposed to happen this way!" Wasn't that what Valerie said? Andrew stared out his bedroom window. What did that mean? So many different options came to mind. Did she mean he wasn't supposed to fall in love with Annabel? Or was it something else? Book detectives made analyzing people's words and motives seem so easy. What he wouldn't give for those skills right then.

What am I supposed to do, Lord? I feel so lost without her in my life. Andrew plopped on his bed and held his face in his hands.

What more could he do but pace and pray?

NINETEEN

After three days of pacing and prayer, Andrew lay across his bed, arm thrown over his eyes, still thinking. He'd been locked up here for three days. He needed to get out of here. The letters, the surgery, Valerie and his parents, it all fit.

Andrew had gathered his notes on the letters and just kept rereading them. Something about the handwriting was familiar to him. When the answer still hadn't come to him, he had paced the room, mulling over the conversation he had had with Valerie and his parents. There was one particular thing that stood out to him and wouldn't let him go.

Valerie had said, "I've worked too hard to make you mine. This isn't what's supposed to happen!"

What did she mean by that? She had worked too hard? What? By making him attend all those events with her?

Andrew's heart had stuttered. The handwriting. He'd seen it before.

Valerie would write little notes to him with the address of the place they'd be going the next day. He hadn't thought much of the elegant scrawl at the time, but the more he had thought about it, the more he realized that it matched the notes Annabel had been receiving.

If Valerie was willing to threaten Annabel to get her way, what else would she be willing to do?

He needed to get these letters to Mark and tell him what he had discovered. He had tried sneaking out the day before, but his father had caught him and sent him right back.

Which brought him to where he was now, lying on his bed and praying for a miracle.

He was answered with the click of his door. He sat up and saw Roger enter the room.

"Mister Andrew," he greeted, holding a tray with a bowl of soup on it.

Andrew's shoulders slumped. "Hello, Roger."

Roger gave a laugh. "That's quite the greeting."

"Sorry, Roger I just hoped I was finally being freed from my house arrest."

Roger walked to the door but stopped before exiting. "Your parents will be back at seven. That gives you nine hours to do whatever you need to do and be back here before they return."

Andrew raised an eyebrow, "You're helping me?"

Roger sighed, "I can see how much that young woman has helped you change and how much you loved and cared for her. Who am I to stand in the way of that?" With that, he was gone.

Andrew jumped up and grabbed his things. He scurried down the stairs and out the front door. Taking his car would be too obvious, so he took off towards Main Street, suit jacket wrapped tight around him to battle the cold air blowing through the city. He hailed a taxi and directed the driver to Mark's office.

The drive was quiet. Andrew did his best not to draw attention to himself lest he be spotted by someone he knew. He could only imagine how much worse his punishment would be if his parents found out he had managed to sneak out. Not to mention the trouble the staff would be in if they were suspected of aiding him. He didn't want to get them in trouble, especially not Roger.

At the office, he paid the driver and let the man go. He'd get another taxi and hopefully keep a low enough profile this way. Stealth was key.

He opened the door and walked into the waiting area. He refused to be kept outside this time.

"You again! You can't just barge in here——" Margaret protested, but Mark quickly cut her off.

"It's quite all right, Margaret. It looks like an urgent matter of business."

Andrew nodded.

Mark gestured toward his office, and Andrew hurried inside. Closing the door behind them, they both settled in the chairs by the desk.

"To what do I owe this visit?"

Andrew pulled the letters from the inside pocket of his suit jacket. He set them on the desk and pushed the packet over to Mark. "Annabel's father found these with her belongings. I also had a rather unpleasant encounter with my parents and Valerie three days ago."

"Oh?"

"Yes, and Valerie said something rather odd."

Mark pressed his fingers together in front of him. "Go on."

"When I told her that I wouldn't marry her now, she was furious!"

"Right."

"But then she said, 'I've worked too hard to make you mine. This isn't what's supposed to happen!'"

Mark sat forward in his chair. "Is there anything else?"

Andrew pointed to the letters. "That's Valerie's handwriting. It took me a bit, but after analyzing it carefully, I realized it was hers. I recognize it from the notes she used to leave me with addresses for the events we attended together."

A broad smile stretched across the investigator's face. "I think we've got her, Mister Andrew." He took the letters and tucked them into his desk. "I'll take these with me tomorrow when I go to visit Mr. Griffith. I think this is just the connection we needed."

He held out his hand to Andrew, who shook it.

"Good work, lad."

Andrew gave his first genuine smile and dipped his head.

"I have to go now. My parents have me under house arrest, and I only have so much time before they arrive back home."

Mark gave him a pat on the back and walked him to the door. "I'll reach out to you when I've got the information we need."

The two gentlemen bade each other farewell before Andrew hailed a taxi to take him back to his street corner. From there, he sprinted home and slipped inside. Voices sounded from the hallway and grew steadily closer. Andrew quickly ducked into one of the niches in the foyer. He maneuvered around the expensive pottery his mother had on display. If it wasn't so imperative he stay quiet, he'd knock it over so they'd be rid of it. How could someone own something so hideous?

Peering around the corner, Andrew watched the new maid Scarlet continue down the hall as she stopped and wiped the paintings along the way. He sneered as she walked out of sight. She was the last person Andrew wanted to run into right now. If she spotted him, he had no doubt she'd make her way to Valerie and spill the beans on his departure. He tiptoed up the stairs, pausing anytime he thought he heard her coming. With a quick stop at the lavatory to fresh up, Andrew was all ready to spend the remainder of the day back on house arrest.

He smiled to himself as he laid on his bed with a book. He was getting the answers he needed.

Now he just needed to find a way to escape the wedding, but he had plenty of time to plan. He wasn't going anywhere any time soon.

TWENTY

The wedding drew closer, and Andrew had only been let out to participate in wedding activities. Mark had managed to slip him a letter through Roger letting him know the talk had gone well, but more questions needed to be answered as a result of the conversation. The note held no details, deliberately left vague should anyone else get a hold of it.

Andrew would be lying if he said he wasn't anxious to know what Mark had discovered. Especially with the note he had received from Mark that morning.

CONTINUE WITH WEDDING NEXT WEEK. PLAN IN PLACE.

Andrew had read the note at least a hundred times. None of the questions that piled up had been answered. He was no closer to finding out what the plan was than he was to discovering what had happened to Annabel. Not knowing what was going on brought on a whole new level of misery.

A knock interrupted his thoughts. "Andrew?" his mother called out.

Andrew sighed. "Yes, Mother?"

"It's time for your final suit fitting. Are you ready to go?"

Andrew tugged his suit jacket on before opening his door. "Yes."

She nodded and started back down the hall. Andrew followed right behind her, not wanting to be accused of anything. They headed out the door and into the car waiting for them on the street. This was Andrew's favorite part of the wedding planning itinerary. He loved just riding in the car and gazing out at the buildings and people that passed by. Maybe it was because he had been cooped up for weeks, or perhaps it was just that he had a new appreciation for how short life could be. He'd venture to say it was a combination of both.

The car came to a halt outside of his father's favorite tailor. Andrew did not like the suit one bit. It didn't fit him right and left him feeling rather like those peacocks that strutted about Central Park.

If this was what his suit looked like, he could only imagine her dress. That thought made him shudder.

He noticed a familiar mop of ginger hair dash around the back of the shop.

"Excuse me. I need to use the facilities." Andrew stepped down from the platform.

His mother pressed a hand to her forehead but said nothing.

Andrew slipped into the back room and searched for the ginger-haired man.

Mark popped up behind him. "Ah, I see you catch on quick."

His sudden appearance made Andrew jump and grab his chest, which prompted Mark to snicker.

"Why are you here?" Andrew asked. "And what's with that note you gave me? What's the plan?"

Mark held a finger up to his lip. "All in good time, my boy. The less you know, the better. It'll make it more believable."

Andrew wished he had Mark's confidence.

"I've learned more after talking to Griffith. This is going to be big." Mark slapped him on the back. "We're almost there, kid. Just give it a bit more time."

Andrew prayed he was right.

THE NEXT WEEK passed in a blur. Before he knew it, his wedding day had arrived.

Andrew had already emptied the contents of his stomach twice. The pressure mounted, and the stress ate away at him. It couldn't end soon enough for his health and happiness.

What if their plan didn't work? Would he have to marry Valerie anyway?

Andrew's stomach rolled. No. He owed this to himself for a change. He'd let them steer his life for too long. It wouldn't be an easy road, but he had people who might be willing to help him. No, he wouldn't marry Valerie. No one could make him do that.

Someone knocked on the door, most likely come to tell him it was time to start getting ready.

"Yes?" Andrew called out.

"Son, it's time to start getting you ready." His father's voice sounded slightly muffled through the door.

Andrew sighed and stood up. He couldn't turn back now. After rinsing his mouth, he opened the door.

"All right, Father." A pall settled over him—one almost as heavy as when he had learned of Annabel's death. Something deep within told him this was the end and that whatever Mark had planned wouldn't work.

He needed to trust the path God had laid out for him. If Annabel could do it, he could. She had faced so much more adversity than he ever had, and through it, she never lost her faith. He wanted that kind of faith.

He followed his father into the room where they started dressing him and slicking his hair to the side.

Andrew forced down the bile creeping up his throat.

They ushered him down the stairs, out the door, and into the car.

Time whizzed by as if on a speeding roadster. How could they already be on their way to the church? His stomach rolled, and nausea crept up his throat once more. The sight of the church made the sensations worsen. He felt guilty for the reaction, but he knew the feelings weren't directed at the place, just the event about to take place.

Andrew dragged his body up to the altar where he could only stand and wait. Guests had started to be seated in the pews, and excited chatter filled the air. He could hear the shouts of joy outside the doors and knew what that meant. Valerie had arrived. Everything would change within the next hour or so, but Andrew still didn't know what that change would look like.

He could only pray Mark knew what he was about. He had to trust Mark's word—trust, even, that God might be using Mark to accomplish His purposes. There was a plan, and hopefully, everything would go according to it.

Annabel danced across Andrew's thoughts as the door opened. All he could think of was Annabel in a beautiful white dress being wheeled down the aisle with her father behind her every step of the way. Andrew was ripped from his daydream as Valerie in her gown appeared at the end of the aisle. He'd never seen something so awful in his life. She looked sickly in her ivory dress that reflected hues of pale greens and yellows. The silver beading that adorned it just made it gaudy. Not the dream bride a groom would envision. A part of him felt bad thinking it, but it was the truth.

As Valerie reached the altar, a frown pulled the corners of his lips down, but he quickly put on the happy groom mask before his father scolded him.

The minister began to speak, and Andrew began to pray.

The time had come.

TWENTY-ONE

Andrew didn't catch a word the man said as the ceremony began. He hadn't spotted Mark enter the church, and his confidence waned.

The officiant droned on and on. Andrew became certain that he would have been bored even if he had wanted this wedding. He vaguely heard something about "forever holding your peace" before a man in the back stood up and yelled out. Andrew whipped his head in the direction it came from. A familiar mop of red hair came stalking down the aisle. Murmurs and gasps echoed throughout the room.

"What is the meaning of this?" his father called out.

Mark gave a smug grin. "I object."

Valerie's parents stood up and marched over, Andrew's own mother joining as well.

"Who are you?" she asked.

Mark pulled out a card and handed it to her.

"Mark Westley, private investigator."

The two couples examined the piece of paper. Andrew wanted to melt into a puddle of relief. He wouldn't have to refuse to do this.

"I was hired by my client to find the whereabouts of his dead girlfriend," Mark gave a nod to Andrew who returned the gesture.

More noise rose up from the crowd, but the two sets of parents and Valerie looked at him in shock.

"What?" His mother stepped closer to him.

Mark continued. "He came to me and told me how his girlfriend had been killed, said she'd been offered an operation, and never made it out alive. On top of that," he pulled out a set of papers, "he also learned that she had been receiving these threatening notes."

Mark stepped forward. "He wanted to know who had paid for the operation and who had sent the notes. Well, I've gathered evidence, and I know who the culprit is."

Andrew looked around at everyone there. "Valerie?"

She fanned herself with her hand looking pale. "It's rather warm in here. I need a bit of fresh air." She turned around, but Mark caught her arm before she could leave.

"Hang on there, miss." He gave a slight tug, and Valerie rejoined the group.

"What is the meaning of this?" Valerie's father asked, rather indignantly. "Unhand my daughter!"

"Sorry, sir, but I can't do that. She's going to the authorities."

"What? Why?" Valerie cried out, tugging against Mark's hold.

Mark tightened his grip. "Do you want me to tell them, or do you want to confess?"

"I don't know what you're talking about!"

Mark sighed. "It would have been better for you to tell the truth. I talked to Griffith. He turned on Miss Porter here rather quickly."

Andrew faced her. "It really was you? You offered her the operation? You knew how dangerous it was!" His body shook with the force of the anger coursing through his veins.

How dare she do this to Annabel! Annabel had done nothing to her to deserve this. Tears streamed down Andrew's face. He didn't care how it looked to those present. "Why? Why did you do it?"

Valerie rolled her eyes. "You're mine, and she was getting in the way! I knew you'd get over her eventually, and then you'd be all mine."

Andrew scoffed. "I was never yours. I've never held any interest in you. Nothing you could have done would change that." Andrew took a deep breath. "All you've done is ensure that I will never love you. You are one of God's creations so I do not hate you, but I could never love you."

Valerie screamed and charged him, but Mark pulled her back. Andrew wanted to laugh as she didn't make it very far.

"You took Annabel from me, Valerie. You killed the woman I hoped to marry." Andrew took a step closer to her. "Despite that, I forgive you." Andrew looked down at the woman in front of him. "It's what Annabel would have wanted, and I want to honor her memory."

"She's not dead."

Mark dropped the bombshell, and the room went quiet.

It took a few moments before Andrew could speak. "What?"

Mark smiled. "You were lied to. Annabel survived the surgery."

Andrew grabbed Mark's shoulders. "Where is she?"

Mark's smile slipped a little. It made Andrew's stomach clench. Why did Mark react like that?

"Mark, where is she?" Andrew asked again.

The older man sighed. "I don't know. Someone picked her up from the facility, but I don't have any record of her after that." He set a hand on Andrew's shoulder. "I'll find her lad. Just have faith."

Andrew nodded. He felt close to bursting at the emotions that surged through him. She was alive! His little mermaid wasn't gone. He wanted to fall to his knees. Relief flooded his veins, and a huge smile spread across his face.

"There's no point. You'll never see her again. You'll marry Valerie and that will be the end of it. Do I make myself clear?" Andrew's father cut in between the two men.

Andrew glared at him. "No, Father." He took a step forward. "You've steered my life for long enough. I will have no more of it."

The man's nostrils flared. "How dare you—"

"No, Father. It's over."

His father's laughter chilled him to the bone. "If you go through with this, you'll never be welcome in our home again."

"I think we can help with that."

Andrew whipped his head towards the entrance of the church. There stood William and the troupe, all with smiles on their faces.

"Who are you, and what do you think you're doing here? You weren't invited!" Valerie's mother shrieked at a frequency that made Andrew's ears ring.

"I did." Mark answered.

The group turned to look at him.

"I suspected this might happen, and well, they deserved to know the truth as well."

William came forward and pulled Andrew into a hug, clapping him on the back. "You're always welcome with us. We can look for Annabel together."

Andrew smiled and wiped the tear that dripped from his eye. "I accept, if you're sure you'll have me."

William returned the grin. "Welcome to the family!"

The troupe cheered behind him. Andrew hadn't felt this happy since before Annabel disappeared.

Annabel. Knowing she was alive made Andrew's stomach flutter and his heart rev with the force of the strongest motor he'd ever driven. She wasn't gone.

Now, he just needed to find her.

TWENTY-TWO

Andrew had never run so fast in his life. When he got the latest update from Mark, Andrew had dropped everything and took off for the Kings Park State Hospital. It took him a couple hours to drive up there, but he didn't regret a minute of it. Not if he could have her back in his life again. Not if he could save her from what awaited those who lingered in places like that for too long.

As soon as his car was parked, he jumped out of the vehicle and ran. She would not be a captive here any longer.

No amount of inquiries or bribing was enough to make the nurses talk. None of them had ever heard of Annabel, but Andrew would not leave without investigating on his own. He ducked around the corner and watched them walk down the hallway. Not able to see them anymore, he slipped into the main hallway. But luck wasn't on his side.

"Hey!" someone called out to him.

Andrew didn't bother to look back. His heart thumped aggressively against his ribcage as he raced down the halls. This is where Mark's letter said she should be. He had searched every corner of the city—the state even—for so long, and now he was so close. She had to be here.

A sharp pain shot through his side, and he took deep breaths as his feet slammed against the ground. He needed to keep going. For her family. For himself. For her. He dashed past door after door toward the light coming in from the end of the hall. For a part of the country that saw so much sun, the halls of this place were dark and rather cold. How did the patients not get sick often?

Now was not the time to dwell on these thoughts. He had to keep pushing. She was within his grasp, and nothing could keep her from him. Not anymore.

Orderlies called out and chased after him. He didn't dare stop.

The scuffing of his leather-soled shoes hitting the white tiled floor echoed off the drab walls, drowning out whatever they were shouting. Not that Andrew was listening particularly hard anyway. He kept his steady quick pace: left, right, left, right, left—his foot hit the ground wrong, and he tumbled onto the tile. Arms shooting out in front of him, Andrew braced for impact. His wrists jolted as they collided with the solid floor. He held his chin up to keep it from cracking with his crash.

Andrew pushed himself up as quickly as he could, not bothering to dust himself off or straighten his clothes before he took off for the doors once more. The orderlies had gained on him during his fall. He needed to move faster. He must not give up now. Though his body protested the strain against it, he continued to push himself harder.

The door to the activity yard was in his view. Just a few more feet, and maybe he would be able to set his gaze upon her again. She could be just outside that door. He was so close. Just a bit more.

Using the momentum Andrew regained after his slip, he gave the double doors a violent push, and they banged against the walls behind them. At that moment, he couldn't care less about the doors or even the orderlies behind him. He searched

for the familiar head of flaming hair, but she wasn't there—
she wasn't anywhere. His heart dropped and panic settled in
his chest. Were his lungs constricting too? She should be here.
He was told this was the last place she was seen. Was it a lie?
Had she even been here in the first place? No. Andrew
couldn't give up hope just yet. He would search for her until
he found her.

Andrew ran from person to person, staring into each face
and examining their features. A few patients protested, but he
kept looking, hoping to find the one face he was desperate to
find. No luck. Andrew was just about out of time. He could
hear the orderlies slam through the same set of large wood
doors. He surged onward. Nothing they did would stop him
before he'd completed his mission. He weaved through the
patients, continuing his search. She had to be here.

Finding her was all that mattered.

Lord, please let me find her, Andrew prayed.

It was a lesson he treasured. *"The Lord hears the pleas of His
children, Andrew."* She would stop and pray when she was
thankful, sad, or hurt. Hearing and seeing her pray had
inspired him to do the same, and he hoped the Lord would
answer this one.

He reached the end of the large grassy courtyard and
came to a stop in front of a woman in a wheelchair. The
young woman sat by herself under the shade of a weeping
willow tree. A thick wool blanket was tucked firmly around
her lap, and a greatly used book lay open upon it. The pages
were worn and discolored from overuse. There was something
so familiar about her the more he looked at her. Approaching
her with caution, he knelt down before the girl. He only knew
one woman in a wheelchair. He didn't want to give himself
false hope, but it was too powerful to quell. She looked into his
eyes, and he knew. She was right here in front of him.

Andrew had not recognized her by her hair, for it differed
greatly from the last time he'd seen her. No longer fiery red,

but a soft dark blonde like the faded pieces of hay she was always surrounded by in her tent. But those eyes. *Her* eyes. He knew those vibrant, emerald-green eyes. He'd spent enough time gazing into them when he was with her.

He called her name, voice barely above a whisper. "Annabel."

Tears pooled in her eyes and trailed down her face. "Andrew? Is that you?" she sniffed. "Is it really you, or am I dreaming again?"

He grabbed her hands in his. "It's me, Annabel." He gave her fingers a gentle squeeze. "I've come to take you home."

He brought her close to him, embracing her tightly, as if she'd disappear again if he let her go. She threw her arms around his neck and sobbed against him. "I missed you so much."

"I missed you too." He pulled back and looked down at her, wiping her tears away.

A wide smile spread across her beautiful face, and Andrew almost melted.

"Let's go home, Andrew."

He had found her. His little mermaid.

EPILOGUE

A ndrew stared down at the newspaper in his hands. His parents' picture was showcased on the front page. GRAYSONS DISGRACED AFTER CONNECTION TO THE PORTER SCANDAL stood out in bold print right above the picture. He was grateful that he had managed to get out when he did. He'd rather not be caught up in that drama.

He never imagined that Valerie would be willing to throw someone else's life away so casually. Worse than that, his own parents had lied without hesitation about Annabel's death. His blood still boiled at the thought of them having her institutionalized. For once, justice was being served. He just wished it hadn't taken so long for his parents to be implicated in the mess.

The sound of a tent flap caught his attention. Blonde hair draped over his shoulder and arms wrapped around him.

"Anything interesting?" a soft voice asked.

He looked back and smiled. He wasn't quite used to seeing her naturally blonde hair, but he loved it just the same. He loved *her* just the same. After all they had been through, he sought to capture every happy moment he could with her.

After the events with Valerie and his parents, Andrew had

suggested the troupe head out West with their act. They needed to get away from the city that had housed so much strife.

With that plan in mind, he had pulled all of his funds from the bank. The moment they were far enough away from the clutches of his family, he and Annabel had finally wed.

Now, not only was he officially a part of the family, he was also now an official part of the business. Though her legs were no longer conjoined, Annabel could still put on an incredible mermaid performance. William and Andrew had struck up a partnership, and Andrew had become their benefactor.

Sometimes he missed the sights, sounds, and smells that had once been such a comfort to him. But as he looked down at the little boy in his wife's arms, he couldn't bring himself to regret any of the decisions he had made. Every single one had been a stepping stone to his present life, and he wouldn't want to change it. His little mermaid had overcome the many difficulties in her life and had swum her way into his life and heart.

There was nowhere else he'd rather be.

The End.

ABOUT THE AUTHOR

Denise L. Barela is a twenty-something-year-old writer with a passion for fiction, her faith, and just being creative in general. When she's not working away at her desk, you might find her reading a good book or following Alice down the rabbit hole...

facebook.com/AuthorDeniseLBarela

instagram.com/artisticnobody1996

pinterest.com/artisticnobody

amazon.com/author/denise-barela

bookbub.com/profile/239822666

BOOKS IN THE EVER AFTER MYSTERIES SERIES

SLASHED CANVAS

A SNEAK PEEK AT THE NEXT EVER AFTER MYSTERY!

LIZ TOLSMA

ONE

Paris, June 1923

The painting spoke to her. From inside its gilded frame, it whispered to her of home. Of golden fields of grain waving in the summer's breeze, of palaces bright with blazing light amid the darkest days of deep winter, of whirls of colors encircling the onion domes of churches where bells rang in jubilation.

And now those bells tolled for the death of all she loved. The fields lay cut and fallow. The palaces echoed, dark and cold. The churches empty, their bells mourning the passing of the old way of life.

Princess Katarina Volstova sighed and shifted on the padded bench in front of the large painting displayed on the Louvre's hallowed *salle rouge* wall, the red rich and deep, covering every surface of the long gallery. Gold-painted swags and medallions covered the coved ceiling, and a gold frame enclosed a massive glass skylight that shone light into the gallery.

But it wasn't the beauty of the room that capture Katarina. Her sole focus was on the work of art in front of her.

Dmitri Popov was a master. Each of his brush's strokes across the canvas captured Russia in all its glory.

The painting itself was simple. A lane lined by birch and aspen trees, bare against a vibrant pink sunset, ran in front of a thatch-roofed cottage, smoke curling from the stone chimney. Along the road, a peasant labored under the burden of a bundle of sticks, a scene she had witnessed a thousand times herself as she traveled in her carriage from her summer home to the Winter Palace, trunks of clothes weighing down the conveyance.

Alexander always sat beside her.

The all-too-familiar pain sliced through her heart. Her beloved, her very heartbeat, stolen from her by rebels who hated him for the station in life he'd been born to. He'd never done them any harm. If they had taken the time to know him, they would have found him to be kind and gentle and respectful of all.

Instead, they struck him down in the street in front of their house, his lifeblood mingling with the melting snow, staining the hem of her gown when she cried and prayed over him.

To no avail.

Katarina choked back a sob.

Because of those brutes, her twin daughters, born in French exile short months after Alexander's death, would never know their father. He would never bear them on his broad shoulders or brush his whiskered cheek against their smooth ones. They would not remember him calling them *moya malen'kaya lyubov'*, my little loves, while they still grew inside her.

Today, those children turned six. How could it be that so much time had passed when the events that brought her here felt as if they happened only yesterday? Katarina had little heart for celebrating the occasion, another reminder they weren't the family they should have been. Perhaps if she purchased them each a frilly new dress, and a dollhouse filled with miniature furniture, it would be enough that they wouldn't miss having a party.

If only she could turn back the hands of the eternal clock and step inside the painting to a different time. She would have drunk in every moment her feet trod Russian soil. She would have loved Alexander better and more. She would have not taken life the way it had been for granted.

Behind her came a squeak. This sound now was also forever ingrained in her mind. The squeak of the janitor's bucket on wheels as he washed the herringbone wood floors.

It meant one thing. The end of her day in the Louvre and her trip back in time and place. It meant her need to return to the reality of life in exile in a city that could never compare to Moscow or Saint Petersburg. Though the communists had changed its name, the city of her birth would never be Leningrad.

"Excuse-moi, madame. It is closing time." This janitor's voice was different from the usual one.

She turned on the bench. But it wasn't the old man who usually warbled those words. Today the man was young. No older than she was. Fair-haired, blue-eyed, and broad-shoul-dered. As straight and tall as the trees in the painting.

She cast her gaze over him. He was missing his left leg. Another war invalid. Another casualty of the insanity that had gripped the world less than ten years ago. He stood with a crutch tucked under one arm, maneuvering his bucket and mop with the other.

She rose, her joints as stiff as if she were fifty, not two decades younger than that. *"Oui,* I know my time is up. I am going." Her voice rang in the long chamber. She stared hard at the man.

Wait a minute. He lived in her building. A boutique occu-pied the first level. There were several smaller, simpler flats on the second and third levels, while she occupied the penthouse on the uppermost floor. He often spoke to her girls with a genuine warmth and kindness that few possessed. His name. His name. Why couldn't she remember it? "You live in the same building as I do. And now you are the janitor here?"

"I am. Georges Velvey."

Da, that was his name.

"And you are the foreign woman with the twin daughters."

"I am Russian." She drew herself to her full height, though she still would only come to his shoulder.

"Ah. Well, I hope you've enjoyed your time at the Louvre." He brushed a dirty blond lock of curly hair from in front of his deep blue eyes.

"I always do. I come every day, just to see this painting. It reminds me of home. Of the Russia I left behind."

"My friend, Henri LeValle, who used to be the janitor here, told me that. I suppose that means I'll see you again tomorrow."

"What happened to Henri?"

"He retired. He'd been washing the floors here for more than thirty years and finally decided that it was time to spend more time with a paintbrush in his hand."

He too lived in their building, so she saw him not only in the museum, but also at her residence. He wasn't as kind to the girls as Monsieur Velvey, but he was always good to her. "I shall miss him. It is strange that he didn't mention his impending retirement to me."

"He is a private person."

That much was true. He never shared about himself when he entered the *salle rouge* at the end of each day. "He allowed me to stay a few extra minutes so I could say goodbye to the painting each night."

Monsieur Velvey nodded. "I've forgotten your name."

"Princess Katarina Volstova." No matter if the title gave others the impression she was putting on airs. She would never relinquish it.

"A princess?"

"That is correct. And now, I must be on my way home. My daughters are waiting for me. It's their sixth birthday." The sixth time they celebrated without their father. And why she was telling this to Georges the janitor, she had no idea.

To compensate for her oversharing information, she raised her chin and swept from the room, the heels of her white T-strap shoes tapping on the floor.

As soon as she was out of his sight, however, she wilted. She was fooling no one. She was no longer a princess. Her royal pedigree meant nothing anymore. She was but a Russian refugee in a foreign country, attempting to give her daughters a life.

The walk from the Louvre to her apartment on Quai de la Mégisserie on the edge of the 1st arrondissement wasn't far. All too soon, she left behind her daydreams and her memories and stepped into the crowded street. She made her purchases for her daughters and, with a clerk following with her packages, made her way along the Seine to the place she now called home.

Nothing as grand as what she was used to, but this neoclassical building with giant arched doors, long windows, and elaborate iron grates that made up Juliet balconies overlooking the Seine was what she could afford. Besides, they didn't open up palaces for refugees.

Once upstairs in her flat, Celeste, the older woman who served as the girls' nanny, appeared from the nursery. "Good. You're home. Those children of yours, madame, need a swift kick to their behinds. Miserable, spoiled girls." She muttered the last part, but Katarina didn't miss it.

Katarina directed the store's clerk where to set the wrapped gifts, tipped him, and showed him the door, then turned back to Celeste. "They are just excited because it is their birthday. You must remember how fun that day was when you were a child." She did. Each and every glittering party, first her father and then her husband, had showered her with. The gifts, the food, the music.

"I don't know how much more of this I can take."

"*S'il vous plaît,* you can't leave us." They had been through too many nannies to count. Katarina couldn't lose another one. She didn't have the energy to hire anyone else. "The girls adore you. I promise, I will speak to them and urge them to behave better."

She made her way down the hall to the nursery. "Olga, Anna, Mama is home. And guess what I've brought for you." The girls burst from their room and sprinted down the hall. They didn't greet her. Instead, they headed straight for their gifts.

"Now, now, we must wait until we've had our dinner before we open the presents. There is plenty of time." The odor of roasting chicken wafted from the kitchen. Justine, the housekeeper and cook, had prepared a wonderful meal for them. Katarina's stomach rumbled. She often didn't eat anything until supper time.

The bang of the door announced Celete's leaving. Maybe escaping was a better word.

"*Non.*" Olga stomped her foot, the large blue ribbon in her hair bouncing with the motion. "I want to open my presents now. And you can't stop me."

"Me too." Anna went along with everything her younger-by-two-minutes sister said and did.

Before Katarina could stop either one of them, they had torn into the paper. Pink gift wrap littered the herringbone wood floor. "This dress is mine." Olga held up the purple one.

When Anna lifted the lid on the pink dress, she stuck out her lower lip. "That's the one I wanted. Give it to me." She grabbed at the violet fabric in her sister's hand.

Olga pinched Anna. "It's mine. I always wear purple. It's prettier on me than pink."

Which was laughable since the girls were identical. They

had inherited their father's dark hair and eyes, her rounded chin and high cheekbones.

"I want purple this time." Anna proceeded to chase her sister around the flat.

"That's enough." Katarina's admonition fell on deaf ears. The chaos continued until both children were rolling on the floor, pulling each other's hair.

At last, Katarina caught them. Even though they scratched her face as she kneeled between them, she finally separated them. "That is quite enough from both of you. Don't make me have to punish you on your birthday."

"You never punish us, Mama." Olga's voice held a haughty tone. One that scraped on Katarina's nerves.

And that was the problem. She didn't discipline the children. But how could she? They had been through so much, had lost so much, she didn't have the heart. "I will. One of these days, I will." She stood and brushed her skirt. "Tomorrow, I will return the pink one and get another purple frock for you, Anna. How is that?"

"She can't have one like mine." Olga switched from haughtiness to whininess in seconds.

"It will be different, but still purple. Now, let's go have supper. I am hungry, and I know Justine left a special treat."

With a shriek, the girls raced to the dining room.

Hours later, the girls asleep at last in their beds, the apartment as quiet as the woods on a winter's night, Katarina stared out the window at the Parisian scene below. How could her life have turned out like this? No wonder she needed to escape every day.

She loved her daughters, but they were going to drive her crazy. She might end up in the insane asylum. They needed a father's firm guidance, but Katarina had no heart to marry again.

Alexander had been her everything. There would never be another for her. When he had died, so had she. When they had lowered him into the ground, they might as well have dropped her cold body alongside his.

What was she going to do? How could she go on another day?

GEORGES UNLOCKED the door to his small but bright flat on the second floor of a tucked-away early-eighteenth century building. Once his door gave way, he stumbled inside, limping his way to his lumpy couch, and plopped on it.

After a long evening at work, his stump ached. Throbbed, if truth be told. Though he rubbed and rubbed it, the pain lessened only a little. The doctors had prescribed morphine for him long ago in the hospital when the Germans first claimed his leg, but he refused. Too many men became addicted, muddled and useless remnants of their former selves because of that drug.

Not that the world didn't already view him as a useless remnant. Though he did his best to prove them wrong, nothing could remove their pitying stares each time he set foot —one, single foot—outside of these four walls. The only job he could get was as a janitor. The Louvre was a step up from the place he had been working.

A far cry from the life he'd imagined for himself a decade ago.

He turned toward the easel jammed into one corner of the single room he called home. If only he could sell a few of his paintings, he might be able to support himself, might make a decent living that didn't involve washing muddy footprints from the hallowed halls of a museum that had once been like home.

He sighed and sliced himself a piece of bread from the baguette he'd purchased on his way home in the early morning light. That was one advantage of working overnight.

He was the first one at the boulangerie in the morning and got the freshest bread in all of Paris.

As he bit into the soft piece of food heaven, he couldn't get the image of Princess Katarina from his mind. No doubt about it, she was one of the most beautiful women he had ever met. But those deep brown eyes of hers didn't sparkle in the gallery's incandescent lighting. And she didn't smile. At least, not when she spoke to him.

When she had gazed at the picture, *The Idyllic Life* by Dmitri Popov, a soft smile teased her lips upwards, her gaze a caress across the canvas. Oh, that someone like her might stare at one of his paintings with such longing and yearning as she did with that one. But to have a piece exhibited in the most famous art museum in the world was a dream out of his grasp.

As was any type of relationship beyond *bonjour* and *au revoir* with the lovely and mysterious Russian princess. The sooner he accepted his life as a janitor, the better. Then again, he'd been trying to do just that for the past four years.

The soft tap at the door jarred Georges from his musings. Making small talk with someone wasn't in his plans for tonight, but he opened the door anyway.

"Henri." Maybe his evening had brightened a little. "It is good to see you. Come in."

The stooped, graying man entered before holding out a paper bag to Georges. "A little treat to celebrate your first day at the Louvre."

"You shouldn't have gone to the trouble." Or the expense. Henri hadn't amassed a fortune as a janitor.

"It was my pleasure. I want you to succeed. Go ahead and open it."

Georges unfolded the top of the bag and peered inside. There lay a single, lilac-colored macaron, perfectly round, perfectly smooth. "You remembered they are my favorite."

"Of course. Who could forget when you rave about how

no one made them better than your sweet mère? Well, this one might not be as good, but it's better than nothing."

"*Merci, mon ami.* I appreciate the gesture. Sit."

Henri lowered himself to the sofa, the springs creaking as he did so. Georges cringed, but he had nothing more comfortable to offer the man. Instead, he sat beside him.

"Tell me how your first day was."

"I'm cleaning floors and dusting display cases. There isn't anything very exciting to report."

"But you got to know someone today." A small twinkle lit Henri's eyes.

"Many people."

"You aren't stupid. You know of whom I speak. Someone you have met before."

"The princess, you mean."

"You make it sound like the title is bitter on your tongue."

And here Georges had tried to keep the sneer from his words. "Not really that she has it, but rather that she flaunts it."

"She is proud of it."

"Why?" Georges settled into the chair, broke the macaron in half, and offered a piece to Henri. For a minute, he chewed, savoring the pâtisserie, the meringue melting on his tongue. "She did nothing to earn it. She was born into it. Or married. Either way, she didn't have to work for it. And yet I slave away to keep my body alive. Though some days I wonder why."

"You have said quite a bit. First of all, don't dismiss her out of hand because of her station in life. It is all she knows. Her world has been upended."

"And mine hasn't?"

"No one's life ever turns out like they planned when they were a child. Times and circumstances change. We change with them, move along with the wave so we aren't consumed by it."

Georges nodded. It was a point. Whether it was good or bad remained to be determined.

"Second of all, each life has worth, no matter the station we're born to or the position we find ourselves in. Look at this room." Henri made a sweeping gesture. "You have filled it with art. You have a great talent. Don't waste it on self-pity. Many men lost legs in the Great War. Many men have drunk from the cup of hardship."

"There is no comparison between what I have suffered and what she has." Georges crumpled the paper bag until it was not much bigger than a marble.

"Don't be so quick to judge. All I will do is urge you to spend a bit of time and get to know her better. What you find out may surprise you."

"I doubt it."

But then a vision of Katarina's brown eyes appeared in front of him. Haunted. What sorrows did she carry?